Jared Anderson can't seem to escape the death of his little brother. Every mistake Jared makes is one his brother, Bryce, never had the chance to. And in a family plagued with resentments and unspoken words ... the pain is getting too much to bear.

Sometimes it was just easier to feel nothing.

Trying to dull his feelings, Jared turns to alcohol and so-called friends, but learns that popularity comes with a price. Caught in a personal war, Jared knows that something must change before he loses himself forever. However, reinventing what was left of him seems like an impossible task.

With the sudden appearance of an unwelcome stranger, Jared begins to wonder if the very person he is running from is the only one who can save him.

A story of change, hope, and the healing powers of a family's forgiveness and love.

GOING HOME

First Edition: June 2013

Published by Veiva Books
1709 West 1375 South
Syracuse, Utah 84075, USA

Interior book design by Bob Houston eBook Formatting
http://about.me/BobHouston

Going Home

By

Jamie Lynn Yeager

Dedication

To Bryce, who is the inspiration
for almost everything I do in my life.
I think about you every day!

Acknowledgements

Writing my debut novel, although very rewarding, has been one of the hardest things I have ever done. I am so grateful for all of those special people in my life who have kept me going with their gentle encouragements. I wouldn't be where I am today if it weren't for my extremely supportive family who have laughed and cried in all of the right places.

To my mom, Deanne Taylor, for writing the beautiful poem included in my prologue. You have no idea how many rough nights your words have helped me through. To my dad, Michael Taylor, for always believing in his children, and my siblings, who are always willing to read the messy first drafts and still have only good things to say. To my Grandmother, Karen Asay, whose editing skills were a lifesaver. And to Cindy Savage, for believing in me and my story.

To my husband, Steve Yeager, for continually pushing me to fulfill my dream and helping with anything I needed, whether it was listening to me when I needed someone to brainstorm with or taking care of our many children so that I could write.

And lastly, to my children: Stephen, Taylor, Payton and Jordyn who have dealt with a busy Mommy these last few months. And to my son Bryce, whose memory has been the driving force for everything involving this story.

Now your sweet spirit can be witnessed by many others.

Prologue

A young, blue-eyed boy sat on the ground next to a small white casket. He plucked petals from a basket of purple carnations and placed them atop the white wood, his chubby fingers working carefully to make sure their edges didn't touch. He was unaware of the whispering small crowd gathering around him. Above, clouds covered the sky promising rain which would be a welcome relief on this hot June day.

Two women stood apart from the crowd, clinging to each other and weeping. A few feet away from them, a white-haired gentleman spoke softly with an adolescent boy who seemed oddly detached, as if he didn't believe any of this was real.

The crowd of mourners took their seats under the canopy where the service was about to begin. A young couple sat motionless in the two center chairs. The woman held a pale blue blanket in her hands; she gently rubbed the fabric while the man stared at the black and white photograph of two tiny feet lying near the casket. An older woman read the words of a poem:

Mommy I know this day
Wasn't what you had planned.
But I'm right here beside you
Holding on to your hand.

My spirit has already gone,
There's so much work to do.
But our Father let me come today
So I could comfort you.

I know you and Daddy love me
And it's hard to see me go.

But that is why we're sent to earth
So we can learn and grow.

I wish I could stay with you here
And play with my brother too.
But for now I'll have to wait
Until your missions are through.

I'll be near when you need me
To wipe away your tears.
To hug you tight and kiss your cheeks
And chase away your fears.

And on the day our Father
Calls you to come home.
I'll be right there to get you
You'll never be alone.

— Mommy I'm Here, *Deanne Taylor*

When the service was over and the guests were gone, the young couple watched as their fifteen month old son placed the last petal on the casket. They walked over, crouched down next to the boy and the three of them said goodbye. When they got to the car, the little boy looked back and all he could see was a tiny white speck in a field of green.

One

My head was pounding.

I could barely concentrate and even the moon's dull glow seeping through my window blinds sent shock waves through my eyes, intensifying the pain. I hadn't yet recovered from the night before, but it had only taken a few minutes for me to decide to go partying again. I figured I would just add it to my growing list of irrational decisions.

I don't know why I always did this to myself. I guess it's because I was expected to. I had a year and three weeks left before I would be an adult and no longer a boy. This meant I still had all the good teenage excuses, "I'm young and impressionable," or "I'm just living my life, making mistakes and learning from them." However, to be perfectly honest I blamed my parents. Actually my dad, I really just blamed my dad.

I shoved my car keys into my pocket, flipped on the light and scanned my room. My eyes stopped on the drum set that sat in the corner, next to the window. I walked to the bass drum and lightly pumped my foot on the pedal a few times. The sound beat time with the throbbing in my head. Four years ago my parents had bought me the drum set, and my dad had vowed to teach me to play. It now sat neglected with a thin layer of dust collecting on its top, and I knew as much about drums as I did four years ago.

"Where's my hat?" I mumbled, kicking around a pile of dirty shirts and a pair of tennis shoes lying on the floor. Besides the heap of clothes, my room was fairly clean. Under most circumstances, it would have been a disaster. Cleanliness just wasn't a trait I was blessed with, however I wasn't an idiot. If my mom came in to clean my room she would find things I would prefer to keep hidden. The glass bottle under my mattress was exhibit one.

My mom grew up with a religious mother, which meant no drinking. I never got to meet my Grandma Miller; however, I have heard enough stories. So even though my mom had stopped going to church, she had adopted her mother's "no drinking" rule. That's why my dad kept his stash at his office. I had stumbled across it once while trying to find a report cover when I was eleven. "You should never touch this stuff," my dad had said. "Your mom would kill me." Receiving fatherly advice was scarce and hard to come by, and from that wise counsel I decided that drinking was something I needed to hide from my mom. Now, besides that, I could find little to no reason to stop drinking.

I whipped my blue comforter from my bed and started searching through my white sheets getting more irritated with every second that passed. I stalked over to my dresser and started digging through every drawer, throwing more clothes onto the floor.

My cell phone started vibrating next to some pills and loose change. I dove for the phone answering it before the ringtone could start. "I'm coming," I said, while grabbing an Advil. "Don't leave without me."

I hung up my phone and decided to look through my baseball bag one more time. Shaking my head I pulled out my navy blue and gold hat. Looking over my room again, my mattress seemed to obviously bulge on the bottom left corner, or was that just my imagination? I quickly gathered the mountain of clothes, and threw them on top of the bulge, just to be safe. I scanned my room one last time, before shutting the door.

"Where are you going?"

I stopped and slowly turned. I had almost made it to the front door. My mom's eyes looked red and puffy. She was sitting on the edge of our coffee table with a blue blanket folded neatly in her lap. I looked toward the kitchen wishing I had gone out the back door.

"Out," I quickly answered.

Her eyes widened, "You just got home, and you missed dinner." She was still wearing her apron and I could smell brownies cooking in the oven. She always baked when something was on her mind.

"My baseball practice ran a little late. Then I stopped by Kim's house."

"It's already six. Why do you have to leave now?" Her dark blue eyes pleaded with me. With all the characteristics I had gotten from my dad; I was relieved that I had her eyes.

"I have something." I pulled my car keys from my pocket.

She stood and placed the blanket on the coffee table and walked over to the sofa. She patted the cushion next to her and motioned for me to sit. "What do you have?"

I looked at my keys and scratched the back of my head. I knew that if I sat down the questioning would begin. I needed to get out quick.

"Mom!" yelled Lynn, from the bottom of the basement stairs.

"Grandpa is trying to get out of bed. He only has his cane in front of him and refuses to use his walker."

My mom looked at me and held up her finger as if to say "we aren't finished yet," then called over her shoulder, "Just one second honey! Tell Grandpa I am coming and to please wait for me."

"Fine," said Lynn. "Grandpa, stay in bed!"

I grabbed the door knob hoping enough distraction had occurred and said, "I won't be too late."

"Wait!" My mom jumped to her feet. I couldn't ignore the panicked look that flashed across her face. "Who are you going out with? What are you going to be doing?"

I looked toward the stairs as my sister came running up them, another welcomed interruption. "Mom, Grandpa wants me to call a guy named George." Short strands of unruly blonde hair fell in front of Lynn's freckled face as she planted her left hand dramatically on her hip. "I guess he now has a plane, which someone named George is fixing and when it's fixed he is going to fly it to pick up someone named Barbara in New Mexico." Lynn's black square rimmed glasses had slipped down her nose, and she peered over the top of them. "Wasn't Grandma's name, Ruth?"

My mom let her head drop and slowly massaged her temples, took a few short breaths and then smiled up at Lynn, "Yes honey, Grandma's name was Ruth, but remember Grandpa is ..."

"Going crazy," interrupted Lynn.

I coughed, as I tried to keep from laughing.

"No, Grandpa Miller has dementia."

"Exactly, he is going crazy," she answered, then paused and sniffed the air. "Are you cooking brownies?"

Ignoring the question, my mom turned to me and I spoke before she had the chance.

"I won't be out too late, it's the weekend, I need to unwind," I said while putting on my baseball cap. "I will be home by twelve."

"He gets to go out?" Lynn flung her hands out, palms up. "Then can I have someone over?"

She was not helping my situation.

"It's getting late, honey, I think we all should stay home." My mom stood, walked over to Lynn, and started playing with her hair. "Maybe we could all play a board game, or something."

My chances of leaving the house were getting slimmer.

"Please can I ask Ashley to come over?"

"Sweetie, she's barely twelve, almost two years younger than you. What about a friend your own age. Perhaps someone from one of your classes?" asked my mom, while tightening Lynn's ponytail.

"She's my only friend." Lynn's expression deceived her. Despite my errant behavior, I had noticed that Lynn's friends had seemed to disappear over the span of a few weeks. She hadn't mentioned anything so I had forgotten about it. Lynn folded her arms, and stared at her feet.

Noticing that she may have struck a nerve, my mom smiled, "Go ahead sweetie." Then looked at me through narrowed eyes, "unwind, how?" she asked.

I tried not to grin. My mom rarely was stern and when she tried to be authoritative it was hard not to bust up laughing.

"I am going to chill at Derek's, maybe play some video games," I lied. "I'll call if I am going to be late." Hoping to end the conversation with that, I opened the door and walked out. I paused on the porch waiting for my mom to follow me and demand more details, but she didn't. I knew she was hurt, her eyes always gave her away. She knew I was lying. I stared at the door, feeling neither relief nor guilt; in fact I felt nothing.

It was easier to feel nothing.

I turned, not bothering to look back and walked to my white Honda Civic parked in the street.

ℵ

"Jared! Ten bucks you won't do it!"

I peered off the rocky ledge. The sun was setting and the warm water of the natural springs below mirrored the red and purple western sky.

"Why don't you come join me," I yelled to Derek as I kicked off my sneakers.

"I'm not as crazy, or as sober, as you," laughed Derek as he raised the six-pack in his hand.

"Who says I'm sober?"

I took off my baseball jersey and tossed it over the edge. The navy blue jersey whipped through the air as a brisk February breeze caught and carried it away from the crowd. My golden number five stared back at me as my jersey landed in the dirt. When I was a freshman and made the Boulder High School baseball team, I had picked that number. Now as a junior it had become more; it was a part of me.

"We're waiting All-Star," hollered Derek. He took a swig from his open can and lifted it in the air. "All-Star, All-Star ..." He waved his hands around him. He was only five foot five, half a foot shorter than I.

"We are documenting this momentous occasion," said Gus, the team's first baseman. Gus and several other students had their camera phones out. "You're going to be all over the internet."

"As long as my dad doesn't see," I mumbled. *If you break an arm you can kiss your college pitching career goodbye*, he would say. I turned my head to spit. Thinking of my dad always gave me a bad taste in my mouth.

"How deep is it?" I asked.

It seemed to only be twenty five feet wide or so and even shorter in length. To my right and two cliffs down was a small waterfall. Since it was early spring, there was a lot of water spilling into a smaller pond which was separated from the larger body of water I was standing above. To the far left of me was an underwater cave. Several people I recognized from school were waiting their turn to enter the hollowed out rock. Smoke billowed from three golf-sized holes in its top.

I had been to these natural springs a few times and getting there still hadn't gotten easier. We had to walk through five miles of rocky desert terrain to get to the springs.

The sun was setting quickly and the crystal blue water was turning black as the cliff's shadow swallowed it up. My phone vibrated against the rocky surface next to my feet.

It was my mom.

I stared at my phone until it was silent. Then walked to the ledge and put my hands in the air. A group of boys cheered loudly, one girl covered her eyes and screamed as I dove off the cliff.

Two

Mrs. Flint sat at her desk. Her gray curly hair was pinned up in a messy bun making the top of her head look like a miniature bird's nest. Her frail frame took up only one third of her chair, and she had to sit on the edge to allow her feet to rest on the floor. She sorted through a pile of brightly colored papers, methodically placing them into piles. Every few seconds she would look up from her desk, her thin lips forming a straight line as she smiled, waiting for her first class of the day to start.

Her psychology class was reputed for being the easiest in the school with the least amount of work. My counselor wasn't exaggerating when she told me that getting into Mrs. Flint's class was harder than trying to get into medical school. Consequently, every student at Boulder High tried to take it. Needing one more elective class, I had lied to my mom telling her that I was thinking of becoming a psychologist. Thrilled that my mind was on something besides baseball, she called the school asking a special favor to get me into the class.

For the past eight months, I had enjoyed easy assignments, little to no homework, and tests that I passed without having to cheat. Somewhere along the way I started enjoying psychology. I also felt that after learning a few behavioral, cognitive and developmental theories I'd be able to diagnose my family's many psychological issues.

I sat on my desk waiting for the class to start. My left leg was perched on Kim Fitzgerald's chair. "Everyone's talking about it," she cooed while running her pointer finger across my black and white converse.

"Kim's right man, I wouldn't be surprised if the whole town finds out about your suicide attempt," laughed Derek, who sat two seats behind Kim. He leaned over the girl who sat in front of him, practically resting his head on her shoulder.

With a heavy sigh she turned to Derek and said, "Do you mind?"

"Nope, not at all," he answered without moving. The girl rolled her eyes and scooted to the opposite side of her chair.

"Seriously Jared, if you weren't so hot to begin with ... I would bet that after Friday night you are now the star of every girl's dreams," Kim said with a smile. "At least you are in mine."

"That hurts, Kim," said Derek as he shoved his fist into his chest. "All this time I thought I was the one making guest appearances in your REM cycle!"

"In *your* dreams." Kim laughed, as she dramatically flipped her long brunette hair.

"I dove off a cliff. No big deal," I said glancing down at Kim's hand that was resting on my knee.

"Ladies and gentlemen, he's even humble," announced Derek in a deep voice.

"Speaking of humble," I said, "what can we do this weekend that will get me even more attention?"

"You could take me dancing," answered Kim leaning closer to me.

"Dancing really isn't my thing."

She had it bad for me. Don't get me wrong, I liked it. And what guy doesn't want a beautiful, popular cheerleader practically throwing herself at him. Last year she was voted "Most Likely to Marry a Celebrity." At this point in time, being linked with me gave her the most attention. She was superficial, but I guess I was, too, because I had liked leading her on, keeping her around until something more interesting came along.

"Well, I know exactly what your *thing* is," grinned Derek. "My parents are leaving this weekend on their cruise."

"Great, we can all party at the Dixon pad. You'll be there right?" asked Kim as she squeezed my knee. I thought about the splitting headache I suffered through all weekend.

Why did I do it?

A few years ago, drinking had been a way to get back at my dad. If he didn't want me to do it, you better believe I was going to! But then, things got blurred, reasoning became hazy.

Why am I still doing it?

As much as I questioned my actions, I knew I was weak. I was a prisoner to peer pressure, too worried about what they would think about me if I didn't. I needed to please the crowd, act the way they would expect me to. Popularity was my lifeline.

"You bet I will," I answered.

I bent toward Derek, who had his fist raised in the air, and smacked it. The girl sitting just below us exhaled loudly. I started to wink at her when out of the corner of my eye I saw Payton Carleton walk into the room. Payton and her family had moved here from Utah at the beginning of the year. There was just something that drew me to her. She was definitely "something more interesting."

My leg jerked to the ground as if Kim's hand had been a hot coal. I could feel her glare burning two holes in the side of my head as I flung off my backpack and slid into my chair. It wasn't hard to notice Kim's growing agitation when it came to Payton.

Am I that obvious?

Kim smoothed the sides of her jean skirt, "Looks like we will have to plan our weekend some other time." Her eyes, narrowing slightly, followed Payton as she walked across the room.

Mrs. Flint walked to the front of the classroom and wrote the word "Change" on the board, preparing to start the class. Derek slunk back into his seat and rested his head on his arm. It wouldn't have surprised me to hear him snoring. Derek could usually fall asleep immediately, which was something he regularly did during Mrs. Flint's lectures. In most other situations I would have followed Derek's example, but this was the only class I had with Payton, and as I said before, I kind of liked psychology.

"We are going to be discussing the Stages of Change," Mrs. Flint said excitedly.

Payton quickly rushed to her seat behind me. I immediately turned around and grinned, "Cutting it a little close aren't we?"

"It must be the rebellion in me," she whispered as she tugged on her pony tail holder. Her thick blonde hair fell to the middle of her back. "My brother missed the bus."

"You," I let my mouth drop and widened my eyes in mock surprise, "rebellious?" I shook my head dramatically, fueled by Payton's quiet laughter.

"Stop, you're going to get us in trouble." She laughed.

"In this class we could get away with murder."

"Very true, however, I actually took this class to learn," said Payton as she pulled a blue binder from the flowered bag hanging from her shoulder. Her pale pink shirt matched the pastel petals on the flowers.

"I am offended," I teased. "I also want to learn."

"Great! Then you should find this topic today particularly insightful," said Payton pointing with her pencil toward the dry erase board.

Mrs. Flint stood on a black step-stool, her arm reaching the upper half of the board. Her hand worked feverishly. "Pre-contemplation, Contemplation, Preparation" and "Action" were each written on the right-hand side of the board, the words "Maintenance" and "Relapse" were written on the left. In neat handwriting below Pre-contemplation, Mrs. Flint wrote, "In this stage people do not believe that their behavior is a problem."

"I never realized you thought so negatively of me," I whispered over my shoulder, pretending to be offended. Conversation always came easily with her.

"This is a no judging zone. I am here to help you with your problem."

My hard façade caved slightly as I chuckled. "I love this girl." I wanted to say.

Mrs. Flint dramatically underlined the sentence she had just written before asking, "How many of you have a habit that you know you should change?"

I raised my hand without taking my eyes off of Payton. Her eyes widened as she stared at me. I couldn't stop the grin that was quickly forming on my lips.

"Now, how many of you are unwilling to make that change?"

I paused. Payton's look had become piercing. My confident smile suddenly felt forced, so I turned to look at Mrs. Flint. I slowly lowered my hand, only to raise it slightly back up.

Mrs. Flint pointed to Derek, who had his hand raised proudly, as she asked, "Have you experienced any consequences yet from the behavior you are unwilling to change?"

"Nope," Derek said loudly.

"Exactly!" Mrs. Flint said. "Are you interested in hearing advice on how to quit your negative behavior?"

"No, I am not," Derek said. He grinned widely.

"Those students with their hands still raised, like Derek," Mrs. Flint went on to say, I looked at my half-raised hand and quickly dropped it, "are pre-contemplators."

I stared directly in front of me at nothing. "If I changed, would you like me more?" I asked quietly. I didn't turn around. I wanted to act indifferent and not show how interested in her answer I really was. I slouched in my chair hoping to come across as confident. Out of the corner of my eye I could see Kim shift uncomfortably in her chair. I wasn't being as quiet as I should have been.

After a few seconds, my impatience took over. I turned to see Payton's serious face. She leaned closer to me and said, "You already know the answer." Then she smiled.

My heart jumped to my throat, unsure if my expression revealed my captivation. I managed to compose myself enough to reply, "But being me is so much fun." Satisfied that I had restored our playful banter, I turned back around.

Payton had a reputation around school, not the kind that Kim, Derek or I had. She was different. She was too good for me. I knew how true my thoughts and her statement were. I knew that she was not interested in my lifestyle choices. In fact she was greatly against them. I did admire her though. At times I thought that she might be worth changing for.

Mrs. Flint cleared her throat, and then enthusiastically pointed to the board, "I would like everybody to quickly write the definition of pre-contemplation down, this week's homework assignment will be to dig down deep inside to try and identify a negative behavior that needs to be changed. I will need everyone prepared for next week when we team up with one of my other classes to do our group projects."

"Can I have a piece of paper?" I turned, gesturing toward Payton's binder. I had made it a habit to never be prepared for the class, just in case I needed an excuse to talk to her.

"You know, one day I won't have paper to give you." She smiled showing her perfectly straight white teeth as she handed me a stack of lined paper, large enough to last me a week.

"We both know that will never happen," I said, then laughed and turned to start copying the notes from the board.

ꟾ

I cut across the thin strip of grass separating the cafeteria from the gymnasium. Our school's mascot, a large eagle with its wings outstretched was painted on the white bricks of the cafeteria's north side. Its talons, almost reaching the cement walkway, were worn and faded. I walked to the west building, dodging students as they made their way to lunch. My locker, along with every upper classman's, was located inside instead of the older, weather-worn ones that were outside. A few renovations had been done to the west building last summer in an attempt to modernize our terribly outdated school, and I enjoyed having a brand new locker that actually opened.

Derek caught up to me as I was walking through the buildings' entrance. "You going to lunch?" he asked.

"Yep, just need to grab my wallet from my locker."

We walked by a couple of sophomore girls who were watching us intently. I smiled and winked at the cutest one. Giggles erupted as they ducked their heads whispering to each other. Derek shook his head then bowed slightly; his hands cupped together. "I have much to learn sensei."

"I don't know what you are talking about," I smirked. "And I wasn't the only one they were looking at."

"You know what, you're right. I am going to go see if they need anything."

"You do that."

Derek walked to the two doe-eyed girls as I rounded the corner. That's when I saw him, the new guy, for the first time. Confused, I stopped, wondering if I had gone down the wrong aisle. However the number on the locker to the left of me proved that I was in the right place. I stared incredulously at the person standing directly in front of my locker. I had never seen him before. It wouldn't have been so weird if he had been blocking my locker while talking to a group of friends, or even distracted by something, but he was completely alone. He didn't have a backpack and he wasn't carrying books. He looked uninterested with his surroundings and was staring directly at me. His blue eyes were completely focused.

I felt uneasy, like an electric current was pulsing through me. *What was this kid doing?* Besides his awkward behavior, he looked like any other high school student. His hair was a few shades darker than mine, although it was much shorter. There was nothing too noteworthy about him. He wore jeans and a white sweater, but he looked at me with such intensity that I was uncomfortable. Unsure about what to do, I looked around, relieved to break from his stare. Not wanting to get into an actual fight, I hesitated. Having a quick temper had gotten me landed in the principal's office more times than I care to share and I wasn't in the mood to visit with Mr. Atwood today.

"What's the hold up?" asked Derek impatiently.

"You didn't last long with those two," I said hoping to change the subject.

"They were all talk, no action," Derek grinned. "If you know what I mean."

I glanced toward my locker. He was still there. A timid smile started to spread across his face. "They must have wanted me then." I pried my gaze from him and looked at Derek.

"You always got to put me down." Derek smiled.

I didn't respond because I couldn't focus. Desperate to get out of the building, I turned my back to the lockers. The electric feeling however stayed, and I could still feel his gaze. It was like he was waiting for me.

"What is going on?" asked Derek shoving my shoulder. "You're acting weird."

"Let's go to lunch."

"What about your wallet?"

"I'm not hungry.

I turned toward the cafeteria. My legs couldn't get me there fast enough. Not waiting to see if Derek followed me, I threw the doors open and walked into the sun. Despite the warm weather my body felt rigidly cold. Blind to the people around me, I started walking, unsure of where I was going. I picked up the pace and nearly tackled a boy, whom I recognized as a junior varsity baseball player, standing in front of me.

"Hey, Jared, how are you?" he asked.

"Good ... um," I struggled to remember his name, even though we had talked numerous times.

"Stephen," the kid offered, unaffected by my tactlessness. "You ready for the game tomorrow?"

"Of course," I answered quickly, wanting to end the conversation. I just didn't feel right. Maybe someone was playing a trick on me. I looked around trying to find someone snickering while holding a camera phone, taping my reaction.

I didn't see anyone.

Maybe I was being stalked. Feeling so paranoid bothered me. I hated when I couldn't control my emotions. Usually it was anger I had a hard time suppressing, but this was something entirely different. I wondered if I should have just hit the guy for taunting me, or whatever it was he was doing. He just seemed so calm, as he waited for me to react. He definitely wasn't scared of me, which bothered me more than I would have liked to admit.

Three

I could hear muffled conversation as I reached the front door. My dad's deep voice sounded tense and angry. I glanced at the time, desperately trying to find someplace to be besides there. My baseball bag seemed to double in weight bearing down on my sore right shoulder. I had pitched more that practice than I would have liked, and now I needed to ice it to keep it loose and ready for my game the next day. Unable to find a good enough excuse to leave, I flung the front door open. I used to try and sneak past the altercation; however, quickly realizing that on most occasions I was the subject of the feud, I learned to face it. I didn't need to agree; all I needed was to amuse him then move on with my life.

My dad spun around stopping mid-sentence, his face livid. I had a hard time remembering my dad look at me any other way. This time he made an attempt to collect himself, trying to look as poised as possible.

He hated losing control.

"You came at the perfect time. We have a few things we need to discuss with you." He was all business.

"Oh! You want to discuss something?" I mocked, intentionally pouring on the sarcasm. "For a second I thought you were going to just yell and demand things." If I was going to get punished for something, I felt I needed to make it worth my while. Pointing to my dad's clenched fists, I smirked, "I really know the right buttons to push ... don't I." His knuckles turned white.

My mom was standing next to my dad. Her hands were out in front of her, like she was preparing to stop a freight train from demolishing her. When it came to confrontations in my house you never really knew what could happen. I guess my mom was preparing herself for the worst.

"I have had it with you, Jared," my dad's voice raised an octave.

"What exactly did I do this time?"

"Everything!" he screamed.

"Well that narrows it down."

I flinched slightly as my dad's rage intensified, however after a second I gained composure and pulled out my phone trying to act impatient.

"You will no longer disrespect me, you will dump your loser friends, and you will make curfew."

"So let me get this straight," I laughed, "you are mad because you don't like my friends and last night I came home a little late?"

To be honest I was relieved. I was certain he had found out about the stunt I had pulled the night before. Obviously angered by my flippant attitude, my dad took three long strides toward me stopping inches from my face, his finger dug into my chest. "You will learn to respect me," he growled.

I didn't back up or blink, I held my ground. My heart pounded angrily in my chest, as I whispered, "Or?"

"Michael, let's just take a second to relax and calm down." My mom came and stood next to me. Her hands were on my shoulders. I felt her whole weight on me, as if she was hanging on refusing to let me go. I cringed from the shooting pain in my shoulder.

"Perfect," I thought, feeling more than a little guilty, knowing that in a matter of seconds the focus would be off of me. My mom never learned her lesson; she always stepped in at the wrong time to defend the wrong person.

"Calm down?" His finger dug a little deeper into my chest, "Do you hear our son's total lack of discipline?"

"I know. I just feel that things would be better solved if we weren't yelling. We don't want to end up saying something we don't mean." I was amused at her use of the word "we," since my dad seemed to be the only one yelling.

"Kate, you need to stop defending him all the time … he needs to face the facts." His gaze shifted to me, "I will kick you out."

My mom's head began shaking. She clung more desperately to my baseball jersey. "No," she begged. "You don't mean that."

"Yes I do."

I broke free from my mom's grasp and took a few small steps backward, aware that my parents most likely wouldn't notice if I left the room. Both of their attentions were solely focused on each other. I watched my mom. She had unconsciously pulled the small blue blanket from the wooden box on our fireplace mantel and was twisting it nervously in her hands.

"I will not lose him, I will not let you chase him away," a sob escaped as she spoke. Fully aware that they were now oblivious to my presence, I started to walk to the kitchen. "He is the only son I have left."

I knew I wasn't getting kicked out anytime soon, at least not until I turned eighteen. My dad always made empty threats. Before turning the corner I looked at my mom. She had found her favorite sitting place and looked defeated as she sat in her mom's old rocking chair, the blue blanket in her lap. She covered her face and spoke quietly, "I can't lose another son." I believe it was more to herself than anybody.

My dad stood awkwardly in the middle of the room, his back was to me. He shifted impatiently, "Maybe you should go see a therapist, he … it's been fifteen years Kate. You need to stop living in the past."

She jerked her head out of her hands; a line of mascara had collected under both of her eyes. "You are the one that hasn't dealt with it, Michael." Her voice rose to almost a shriek, "You have never once talked about it. You have never talked about him."

I could easily tell by his body language that my dad was clearly uncomfortable with the way the conversation had gone. He shifted his weight once again.

"It's like you would rather pretend that it never happened," she continued.

"It's done and over with, I don't see a need to think about something that happened so long ago," he said, his voice completely emotionless, except for when it cracked on the last word.

"*You* may want to just forget about him," she whispered, barely audible. "But all I want to do is remember."

Standing, she folded the blanket and set it neatly on the chair, wiped at her eyes and walked out of the room. Not wanting to have to face my dad, I quickly walked into the kitchen. On the marble counter top sat my dad's briefcase and a small luggage bag. I wasn't sure if he just got home from a trip or was leaving, but hoped he was leaving. Most the time I never knew exactly where my dad was. In a family that ran on little to no communication, tracking each other's whereabouts was next to impossible.

Since my dad was a regional vice-president for Hartford Mutual Funds; he was rarely home. He had a few clients who lived in California and usually flew out there once every month to meet with them, take them out to fancy restaurants and try to get them to invest more of their money. He had an office in Henderson, the city directly north of Boulder, but spent a lot of his time driving the thirty minutes to Las Vegas to meet with his other wealthier clients.

I threw my baseball bag into the laundry room, grabbed a gallon of milk and started drinking out of it. I was lucky that my mom had gone to her room and wasn't present to witness the guzzling. Inside the refrigerator was a dish covered in foil with a sticky note on top that read, "Grandpa's dinner." I took it out and knowing that dinner would be a "fend for yourself," thing, I grabbed four slices of bread, some cheese and two Twinkies. I ate a banana as I heated the plate full of leftover lasagna then walked to the stairs. As I passed the living room entrance I instinctively looked in. My dad was still standing in the exact spot where I had last seen him, facing the old rocking chair.

I wondered if I should feel responsible. I would have if this had been an isolated event, but it wasn't. Every so often things would build up and then explode. Each time they never really got anywhere with it. They'd just file it away deciding to resolve it later. I ran down the stairs with the food to my grandpa's room. My parents had remodeled and built a bedroom with a private bathroom downstairs when my mom decided to have her dad live with us two years ago.

"Dinner is served," I said loudly, before I noticed that he was asleep in his chair.

He shot up; his eyes were wide with surprise. "Are you trying to kill me?" he yelled, "I nearly had a heart attack!"

I set his hot plate down on the food tray that was next to him. "I'm sorry, Gramps', I didn't know you were sleeping."

"Well, I'm awake now!" he exclaimed as he went to stab the lasagna with his fork, but I quickly stopped him.

"It is really hot," I said, pointing to the plate, "you should wait just a few minutes."

My grandpa stared at me blankly at first then reclined his chair back once again. "Well, maybe I will just rest for a few minutes then," he said.

"Mom will probably check on you in a little while," I said as I walked away. I could hear him snoring loudly before I made it to the top of the stairs. I carried the bread, cheese, and Twinkies with me toward my room, but stopped at my mom's door.

I tapped lightly on it twice then said, "I brought Grandpa's food to him. I don't know if he will eat it ... he seems really tired."

I didn't wait for an answer. I knew I wouldn't get one.

Once in my room I threw the food onto my bed, and flipped on my stereo, desperate to chase away the awkward silence. The house vibrated from the song's deep bass. I made two cheese sandwiches then walked out into the hallway. Balancing a Twinkie on each sandwich I kicked the partially opened door that led to Lynn's room. I hesitated, almost dropping the food. My sister was sitting on her bed with her knees pulled up to her chest. Her swollen eyes stared at me.

I blinked, momentarily blinded from the pink walls surrounding her. Coming from my dark blue walls to her bright room always startled me. She sat on a white comforter; her canopy bed was draped with white fabric. She reminded me of a young girl who thought she was a princess.

"Would the young lady be interested in an appetizer this evening," I asked in a British accent, while holding out her sandwich and taking an exaggerated bow.

She smiled and wiped her eyes. We sat there eating in silence, listening to a *Lifehouse* song that was playing in my room. Lynn picked at her sandwich then nervously asked, "Are Mom and Dad going to get divorced?"

I didn't have an answer. In fact I had been wondering the same question for years. It seemed like the logical solution for two people who just couldn't get along. It wasn't like they were constantly fighting. It was more like they lived separate lives and tried to have as little contact with each other as possible. We sat there in silence for a while letting the question settle in our minds. It was a real possibility. I would be fine with it, but I worried how Lynn would handle our parents divorcing. She had a naïve, endearing quality about her where she believed that we could all be one big happy family. I worried how she would take it when it came to an end, so I felt a need to slowly prepare her, and in my opinion telling her that everything would be okay and that they would work it out would just get her hopes up.

Lynn must have known what I would say. "I have no friends," she stated flatly, her train of thought had suddenly shifted. I wondered if that was what had really been weighing on her mind the whole time.

I looked at my sister. She picked at her toe nail polish, her shoulders were slumped. She looked defeated. I shoved the rest of my sandwich into my mouth. I wanted it occupied because I didn't know what to say.

"I mean, I don't have any friends who go to our school," she said. "Mom was right."

"I thought I saw you around school with that brunette girl from your band class. What was her name?" I snapped my fingers, trying to remember.

"Lindsey."

"Lindsey! That's right," I shouted, too enthusiastically. "I thought you were great friends."

Lynn just shrugged her shoulders. Her cheeks flushed and her eyes moistened as she tried to hold back tears. Dealing with any girls' emotions freaked me out. Sister, or not, I felt completely uncomfortable and unqualified to be giving advice. If that is what a psychologist has to deal with, females pouring their souls out while they hold a box of tissues, I would need to find another alternative if baseball didn't work out.

I moved her sandwich over, and sat next to her on her bed and awkwardly patted her knee. I wasn't sure if she wanted to talk about it or wanted to end the conversation, but oh how I prayed for the latter.

"We ate lunch together every day last week, but then today during band class she wouldn't talk to me," she blurted out, obviously in the mood to talk.

I shifted so I was facing her and started to ask, "Do you think maybe you were …"

"I thought that maybe I was imagining things," she interrupted, "so I waiting for her at our table during lunch, but then …" Lynn's voice started to quiver.

I raised my eyebrows and nodded for her to go on.

Lynn seemed to hesitate. "She just found some new friends."

"Is that all?" I asked, unsure if there was more to the story.

"I know, I know, I'm being a baby," she said. "I just want friends so badly."

I felt guilty. Why hadn't I noticed this sooner? I had assumed that since the school year was more than half over she would have met people. I kicked myself for not being more perceptive. I had gone nearly seven months without realizing that Lynn regularly ate lunch alone. Unfortunately having her eat lunch with me and my friends was not an option. We weren't the type of crowd I would want my sister associating with.

She perceived my thoughts and added, "Don't worry! I don't want to be seen with your weird friends." She laughed, and wiped her eyes. "I'm almost failing Algebra, so my teacher said that he could start tutoring me during lunch."

"That is probably a good idea," I smiled, trying to hide my relief.

"You know," Lynn said shyly, "sometimes I wonder what it would be like if Bryce were here, if he would have been my friend. Maybe he would have eaten lunch with me."

My heart sunk into the pit of my stomach. I felt like a crappy brother, and I hated it. There was so many times like these where I felt such anger toward Bryce for dying. I was now the son and brother who kept screwing up, being compared to the one that never had the chance to. Bryce could be anything in their eyes, the most considerate sibling, and the most obedient son. Instead, they had me.

Lynn's comment was completely innocent, and I had to admit that I had thought about that same thing almost every day of my life, but I never talked about him to anyone. Lynn would talk about him all the time, but I never did. I kept it all in. "Me too," was all I could say. My mind had started racing, reluctantly reliving the times I had ever wished Bryce were here. The many days of playing alone, pretending I was a super hero fighting an invisible villain, playing catch with the brick wall out back. I'm not sure why I even cared. I had grown up fine without a brother in my life.

Suddenly, I realized I was losing my grip on reality, and I needed to get control. I didn't need him and I needed to change the subject.

"Speaking of failing, I have a ton of homework due tomorrow," I said while getting up to walk to my room. "What about you?"

Lynn's smile faded, "I have a test I need to study for, I guess."

"You also need to finish your dinner," I said pointing to her plate.

I walked to my room, grabbed my backpack and walked back to Lynn's room. She looked surprised when I sat on her bed and pulled out my binder. She smiled, then quickly grabbed her backpack and sat next to me.

"I like to have company while I do my homework," I lied.

Four

I hate to admit, I walked toward my locker a little apprehensively. I couldn't avoid it any longer, I needed my wallet. Luckily, I hadn't seen him all day, but wondered if he had decided to lie in wait for me again at my locker. I figured he was new at the school because I hadn't ever seen him before and the school year was more than half over. If he weren't a new student we would have had this creepy stalker situation already over and done with a long time ago.

I asked around about him, but no one knew who I was talking about. It was starting to look like I had overreacted the day before and that I would never see him again. I breathed a sigh of relief as I shoved my books into my locker and grabbed my wallet. I was starving. The sloppy Joe Tuesday special had my name all over it.

Later during lunch Gus stared at me in disbelief. "Breathe man!" he laughed. "I swear you inhaled your entire lunch."

I shoved three fries in my mouth, "I'm so hungry! I woke up late and missed breakfast."

"And first period," said Kim pouting. "I was so bored without you there."

I shrugged.

Around eleven o'clock the night before, my parents had picked up on where they had left off, continuing to yell until one in the morning. When my alarm clock went off five hours later, I threw it across the room. My mom didn't dare come in to wake me up. I heard her get Lynn up and an hour later take her to school. I slept through my first period and half of my second. Unfortunately I had made it to US History in enough time to take the pop quiz. I definitely failed that one.

"You better hope Coach Kline doesn't hear about you skipping first period, especially on a game day," said Derek. He reached across the table and grabbed a handful of fries from my plate.

"Is it any different than sleeping through the entire class?" I asked.

"At least I am present."

"Coach won't find out, and if he does, he won't do anything about it," I grinned at my teammates. "He needs me too badly."

"Low blow," said Gus.

"Oh, where would we be without the legendary Jared Anderson," mocked Derek as he stole more fries.

"Would you quit it? Didn't you hear me just say how hungry I am?"

I shoveled the last of my fries into my mouth, and then noticed Payton leaving the lunch room carrying a red lunch tray. I just caught a glimpse of long blonde hair and a flowered book bag, but knew it was her. I bet I could have picked her out of any large crowd with ease. There was just something very familiar about her. Besides first period, the select few times I caught her walking outside to eat her lunch were usually the only times I saw her during the day.

"Look! I think a fight is starting," squealed Kim pointing to the south side of the lunch room.

A group of five boys stood around a table. I knew four of them from the school's basketball team; my view was partially blocked from positively identifying the fifth person, he wore a white dress shirt with jeans and stood away from the other four. I had a strange feeling that it was the same guy I had been reluctantly anticipating at my locker earlier that day. My only evidence was their similar body types. There were also two girls standing a few feet back. One of the girls pleaded with the boys to stop.

I recognized her.

She was the brunette from Lynn's band class, Lindsey. I stood to get a better look. I couldn't see past the group of boys.

"It's nothing," said Derek disappointed. "It's been a while since we had a good fight at this school." He sat down laughing, "Actually Jared, I'm pretty sure you were involved in the last fight."

"I probably was," I said starting to sit. That was when I heard it. Someone cried out, "Please leave me alone." I would have recognized that voice anywhere. I abruptly jumped to my feet.

"What's the matter," asked Kim quickly, she reached out to grab my arm.

"It's Lynn," I growled through clenched teeth. I kicked my chair, sending it flying into a group of students eating lunch ten feet or so from us.

Both Gus and Kim stared at me, Kim's mouth opened in surprise. I'm pretty sure they had no idea what I was talking about or that I even had a younger sister. Derek however, had known me long enough to know my family. He lunged for me, but missed. I took off sprinting toward the group of boys and to where my sister's voice had come from.

The boy in the middle of the four bent to tie his shoe. It was then that I saw Lynn sitting alone at the table. Her arms were wrapped protectively around her backpack which sat on her lap. She had her hair pulled back and wore a long sleeved purple shirt. She slowly stood, looking too young to be a student at the school.

"Where are you going?" asked one of the boys. He had jet black hair and olive skin.

Lynn looked up at someone who was standing next to her. She squeezed her eyes shut, then wiped them with the sleeve of her shirt. That was when she noticed me. We made eye contact for a brief second and I can only imagine what she saw; me barreling my way toward her, my jaw clenched, eyes red with rage.

My view of Lynn was blocked when the boy in the middle finished tying his shoe.

"Ask us one more time if you can go," said the tallest boy, he towered over his friends by a good six inches.

"Can I go?" I heard Lynn cry.

Without answering, the four boys burst into fits of laughter. One grabbed his side, and rested his forearm on the taller one's shoulder. I ran around the table directly in front of me and nearly tackled a girl walking with her lunch tray. I was fuming. My mind had been made up. It looked like I was going to get into a fight this week after all. I wasn't too far from Lynn; however my mind had enough time to imagine dozens of painful things I could inflict on those five guys, and the more I thought about it the angrier I got. I was so close to them now, I balled my hand into a fist preparing to hit the closest guy in the side of his head.

I couldn't see the fifth guy anymore and wasn't sure where he had gone, which worried me a little because my goal was to take out as many as I could before they realized they were under attack. I was also uncomfortable not knowing exactly who he was or if he was the same stranger who had been staring me down the day before. I couldn't decide if that made me eager or slightly nervous at the possibility of getting to punch him. I was, however, amused with the fact that the remaining four losers had no idea who Lynn was related to, but that in a matter of seconds they would find out.

He had no idea what hit him.

My hand hurt a little, but it felt so good at the same time. The tallest guy of the group dropped to the ground holding the side of his head. His friend, standing to my right, stared at me in surprise. He covered his face attempting to block my punch, but before I could connect someone plowed into my left side, we both fell onto an empty table. My right shoulder smacked the edge tipping it over on top of us. I screamed as my right elbow took the brunt of my fall, pain shot down my forearm to the tips of my fingers. I shoved the table off me with my left arm. The person who had knocked me over had a nasty gash across his forehead from hitting his head on the same table edge. Blood started trickling down the bridge of his freckled nose making the cut look worse.

Derek ran over to me panting, "We have got to get out of here," he said. He had a bruise quickly forming below his left eye. I screamed out in pain again as he grabbed my right hand to lift me. "Please don't tell me you hurt yourself."

I lifted myself up. The olive skinned boy, who had been taunting Lynn, was hunched over holding his stomach and trying to run from two school administrators, while his three other teammates were being escorted out of the cafeteria by Mr. Atwood. The fifth one must have gotten away. Students gathered close to where we stood to watch the action, but no one seemed to notice us, or that I had actually been the instigator.

I scanned the group of people trying to find Lynn. I hadn't seen her leave the table, but I also had been preoccupied. As far as I could tell she had left as soon as I laid the tall guy out. I hoped she had taken advantage of the distraction.

"We need to leave, and now's our chance." said Derek.

Trying not to bring any attention to ourselves, we slowly walked to our table acting like we were spectators who had grown bored of the scenery. Our friends must have gathered to watch the fight because the table was empty except for Kim, who had both of our backpacks in hand.

"I hoped you guys wouldn't get caught," she smiled, and then added, "I just assumed you were an only child."

"Nope," I replied, grabbing my backpack with my left hand. Most of the people I associated with had a very superficial view of me. I never talked about my family and come to think of it, they never asked. Derek must have filled Kim in on the family relation before joining in on the fight.

I pointed to Derek's bruise, "What? You didn't think I could take all five of them?"

"My intention was to get there before you hit anybody. We need to get out of here," he looked around nervously. "Coach Kline is going to take one look at us and then kill us."

I wasn't as worried as Derek was about Coach, but I also was a starter. Derek spent most of our games warming the bench. Getting into a fight would give Coach another reason to overlook Derek when it came to playing time. But my elbow was hurt, and that *did* worry me. It was no longer a sharp shooting pain, but a consistent dull ache. My shoulder felt stiff, I rotated my arm several times trying to loosen it.

"Do you want me to rub it?" asked Kim grabbing my shoulder.

"I'm fine. Derek's right, we need to get out of here." I pulled the hood of my sweatshirt over my head. "We should split up." I walked to the back exit then called over my shoulder, "Kim, take Derek someplace secluded and put some makeup or something on his face to hide the bruise."

I made it through the rest of the day without any problems. No one seemed to place me near the fight at all. From the few times I talked to Derek between classes, he seemed to be having the same luck. His bruise was no longer dark red but turning purple, luckily getting hit in the face with a baseball during practice was a believable excuse. I hadn't seen Lynn at all though. That's why after school I decided to wait by her band locker, hoping to catch her before she walked home.

Lynn ran to me smiling as soon as she saw me, "What are you doing here? Don't you have a game to start warming up for?"

"Yes, it's just a practice game but I wanted to make sure you were okay."

"I'm great!" She set her clarinet in her locker.

"Are you sure?" I bent over looking her straight in the eyes, "At lunch you ..."

"Something did happen at lunch," she interrupted.

"I know. That's why I wanted to check on you. See if you ... maybe, wanted me to drive you home before my game starts." I figured no one dared bother Lynn again, but didn't like the idea of her walking home alone today.

"You know I made a friend?"

"What?" I asked confused. We were definitely on different wavelengths.

"I met a new friend at lunch today."

"Was that before or after you were accosted by those five idiots?"

"Oh, that's right. I thought I saw you. Um ...?" she said, dropping her eyes. She seemed to be unaffected by the incident, it almost seemed like she had forgotten about it entirely. It was strange because usually something like this would have affected her for much longer than a few hours. "It was kind of during, actually," she answered.

"So you got out of there before any of the fighting started?" I asked relieved.

"Yea, my friend actually helped me. Did you fight?"

"I thought you had planned on getting tutored during lunch." My tone sounded more condescending than I intended as I dodged her question. I ran my hand through my hair, I felt agitated.

"I tried to, but the classroom was locked. My teacher must have forgotten that I was coming," she smiled sheepishly. "But now I have someone to eat lunch with, so I will need to figure out another way to bring my grade up."

I was shocked to see her so happy, I had expected to have a completely different conversation. I was a little disappointed that she didn't get to see the fight or that she didn't get to see me fight for her. I wanted to gloat about my heroic afternoon, but she grabbed my hand excitedly and said, "I really should hurry. My friend is waiting for me so we can walk home together. We actually live kind of close to each other."

Lynn made it past most of the lockers then quickly turned around. She cupped her hands around her mouth and yelled, "Good luck in your practice game," then ran around the corner to the front of the school.

Luck was something I would desperately need.

ઙ

Coach Kline stared both Derek and me down. We sat in the dugout, feeling like a couple of ten year olds getting grounded. Coach paced back and forth shaking his head. He would begin to speak then stop and shake his head some more, either he was trying to intimidate us or he really was too angry for words, I couldn't tell which. No amount of makeup could hide Derek's bruise, and after briefly warming up in the bullpen, Coach knew something was up.

"Why are you favoring your right arm?" he yelled at me, finally able to find his voice. "And don't you lie to me boy!"

"Derek and I were messing around and I fell on it," I answered. "But Coach it's just a little sore, I can still pitch."

"Let me guess, your messing around also caused his black eye?" he asked sarcastically, pointing to Derek. No answer was necessary, he was on to us. "You two are lucky those four boys aren't talking. I should march you to the office and turn your lousy butts in." He began pacing again, "But Jared, I need you." Derek cleared his throat nervously. "If I let this slide," we both looked up, "you better do everything I say. If I need help after practice raking the field, you two better be the first to volunteer. If I ask for volunteers to help run my little league practices, both of your arms better be raised. And if I mention that I could use a soda, you both better ask me 'what flavor?' Do you get my drift?"

"Are you thirsty now Coach, because I could run to the closest convenient store," Derek stood, pointing behind him to the parking lot.

"Get out on the field, both of you, and finish warming up with your team," he growled.

I chuckled as Derek sprinted out of the dugout. I grabbed my glove and started heading to the field when Coach Kline caught me by the arm, "I'll give you one inning, if I notice any resistance on your part; I'm pulling you." His voice softened a little, "There's no reason in pushing yourself too far. You know as well as I, that you actually have a future in this sport, so don't end your career now for a preseason high school game."

Our school's bleachers were filling quickly. This surprised me; considering it was just a practice game. We technically hadn't even had try-outs yet, but we had a pretty good idea of who would be on the varsity team. The umpire was getting everything squared away with the coaches as I threw some practice pitches. My changeup and fastball felt solid. Unfortunately, when I went to throw my curveball that same sharp pain I had experienced earlier shot from my elbow down to my fingertips. It was like how I feel when I hit my funny bone but a thousand times worse.

The first inning went by smoothly; luckily we had two pop flies and a grounder to first. I didn't need to throw any curveballs or any heat for that matter. The second inning didn't go so well. We were playing the Foothill Falcons from Henderson and their number four batter was up. He had hit two homeruns his last game and looked like he expected to do the same. My first pitch he sent flying over our team's dugout crashing into the hood of a light blue Hyundai Accent. My next two pitches were balls. Then I threw my curveball hoping to catch him off guard. Pain shot down my arm, the ball landed several feet short of the plate.

Coach Kline called a time out and walked out onto the mound. "You can't hide the pain I saw in your face," he said.

"I can get him, I got this."

"Fine," he said handing me back the game ball, "Take your time ... be smart."

The bleachers were packed now and I felt stressed. As I got into my stance, the batter twisted his bat anxiously. He swayed back and forth then leaned on the ball of his right foot; both elbows were up, waiting for my pitch. I didn't feel nearly as ready as he looked. My shoulder throbbed.

In a matter of seconds he had sent my fastball over the center field fence, giving him three homeruns in a week and their team the first run. I met Coach halfway to the mound handing him the game ball; he didn't need to tell me. I removed myself from the game. Immediately the school's athletic trainer, Joel, began wrapping and icing my arm.

Our team lost by three runs. The trainer recommended I sit out the next game, but predicted that by next week my shoulder and elbow would be healed and I'd be ready to go. I rotated my arm again. It was difficult with the big ice pack wrapped around it. Hoping Joel was right; I grabbed my baseball bag and headed to my car. Sticking around to hear everybody talk about the game was the last thing I wanted to do. I fought my way through the fans, nodding to those who acknowledged my injury and some who still complimented me on the game despite the obvious.

"Jared, you did great!" Kim caught me from behind and wrapped her arm around my left shoulder.

"Everybody seems to be commending me for losing the game for my team," I sneered, shaking my head. "Save yourself the trouble. Either be honest or don't say anything at all!"

Kim flushed and her hand flopped to her side. She bit the inside of her lip and I knew I had offended her. I grabbed her hand and continued walking to my car. "I'm sorry. I'm just disappointed in myself; it's not you." Her ego seemed to recover, because she leaned into me, putting her head on my good shoulder as we walked. I was relieved that she had caught the hint, because we were able to walk in silence for a few minutes.

We passed the unfortunate owner of the blue Accent. She was on her cell phone talking loudly, while running her fingers over the dent in her hood. A girl was climbing into the passenger seat. When she saw us she intentionally paused, waiting for us to get closer so she could glare at me as I walked by, as if I were solely to blame for her friends' misfortune. "That's why I always park way out there." I chuckled, pointing to the far end of the parking lot. Her mouth dropped open. I kept on laughing. Kim stuck her bottom lip out in an exaggerated pout; then smiled smugly at the girl, which made me laugh harder.

"Will you come over tonight?" Kim asked as soon as we reached my car. She quickly stepped in between me and my driver's side door then ran both her hands up my back, and flipped my baseball bag off my left shoulder. It slid partially under an old red van parked next to me. She then clasped her hands around my neck pulling me closer to her as she backed against my car. I didn't resist, she was hard to resist at times.

She pressed her finger to my lips, then said, "Before you answer, I must confess, my intentions are not at all innocent and my parents won't be home until late."

"That's a very tempting offer," I said, clearing my throat. I knew her intentions, she was always very clear when it came to the type of relationship she wanted. Derek thought I was crazy for not taking advantage of the opportunity, but I never felt right about it. I was terribly uncomfortable about the whole situation, and was trying to hide my uneasiness. I guess I am just old fashioned and feel that certain things should be saved for love and marriage. Unfortunately my image of the whole marriage thing was tainted at the time. "I need to get home," I said, taking the easy way out.

Knowing that she would get agitated with the mixed signals I was sending, I decided it was time to leave, hoping to dodge a fight. Kim, however, seemed distracted as she stared off behind me. "I understand," she said, closing the small gap between us. "The least you can do, is give me a kiss."

A kiss seemed harmless enough.

It wouldn't have been the first time we had kissed and her mood was surprisingly pleasant which caught me off guard. She must have noticed the resolve in my eyes, because she grabbed the back of my head and pulled me closer to her. It had been a while, and all the old feelings I had felt for Kim came rushing back. She was a good kisser. Giving in, I wrapped my arms around her waist. Our relationship was getting more complicated with every second we spent kissing. Almost as quickly as she began, Kim stopped. She looked over my shoulder and asked, "Can we help you, or are you just enjoying the show?"

I quickly turned and saw Payton standing a few feet from us; I hadn't seen her crossing the parking lot. It didn't take a rocket scientist to realize that Kim had plotted the entire thing.

"I don't want to interrupt, and by all means feel free to continue," Payton said sarcastically, "but could you move your bag? That is unless you want me to run it over." She looked directly at me, her cheeks were flushed, and I could tell she wanted to be in this situation just about as much as I did. I awkwardly stepped away from Kim and grabbed my bag from under the van.

"Nice ride." Kim laughed, pointing to the chipped red paint on the back sliding door.

"Thank you!" Payton replied with fake excitement.

The tension was thick and I felt like an idiot. I understood that I was in control of my actions. I just wish Payton hadn't been there to witness that specific action. Kim seemed to be the only one not affected by the situation; she smiled smugly as she leaned against my driver's side window, picking at her nails. Her barely existent skirt wasn't much help either.

I threw my baseball bag into my trunk slamming the door. Payton quickly walked to the other side of her car. I didn't want her to leave and without thinking, I asked, "Did you come to the game to watch me?" As soon as I had spoken I realized my arrogant mistake. I wished I could have caught those self-righteous words and shoved them back in my mouth, where they belonged.

Payton paused. "Does it matter?" she asked incredulously. Kim no longer looked at ease. She walked closer to me. I just stood there, unsure if the question was rhetorical or if she was really expecting an answer.

Obviously seizing the moment, Kim determinedly closed the gap between us and planted a kiss on my cheek. "My tempting offer, as you put it, still stands," she said loud enough for Payton to hear. "You know where the key is." Kim ran her finger across my chest then winked at me before waving at Payton and saying that she would see her in psychology class the next day. I watched her strut away toward her two friends who were waiting to take her home. I turned to look at Payton not wanting to visualize what she thought of Kim's implications.

"I'm sorry about that," I said sheepishly.

"There is nothing between us, so what do you have to be sorry about?" asked Payton as she slipped into the driver's seat and started the engine.

"I would like there to be *something*," I said, "so that I could have *something* to be sorry about." I wished I had left off the second part.

Payton laughed dryly, then pointed to the direction Kim had walked, "As long as that stuff is going on, there will never be *something*!"

I had nothing else to say, I watched her shut her door and back out of the parking space. As she was passing me she rolled down her window and said, "By the way, you played horribly today."

Five

Lynn was grinning uncontrollably. She sat on the edge of the passenger seat with her hand on the door looking ready to bolt as soon as the car stopped. Her giddy demeanor was contagious and helped ease the pain I still felt from my stupidity the night before.

After the game I had gone straight home shunning everyone and keeping to myself in my room. My mom came in once to leave dinner. She probably thought my mood was because of what had happened between her and my dad. Their problems didn't concern me. I had my own issues; however, was unwilling to get into a conversation about me. So I let her believe what she wanted. This worked for me up until ten minutes before, when Lynn and I were getting into my car.

"Honey, before you leave, do you want to talk about something?" my mom had asked. Her hair was a mess and she was wearing her bathrobe with pajama pants and had run down our front steps to the curb where my car was parked.

"What?" I asked in disbelief, pointing to her outfit.

"I'm a great listener!" she said cupping my hands in hers. "Just tell me what you're feeling."

I looked at Lynn. She seemed just as confused. "I am fine," I said to my mom, slowly emphasizing each word. She looked lost, like she had planned on me spilling my innermost secrets to her in the driveway. Little did she know that in my head I was ranting about how helpless I was feeling. I felt like I was being pulled in a thousand different directions and wasn't sure which way I should go. Reinventing me, according to the psychology project, seemed like an impossible task, and unfortunately my only reward for doing so, Payton, wasn't likely to care.

"Can we go? Please!" Lynn pleaded pointing to the time on the dash.

My mom wrapped the robe around her and said, "Well, you know where to find me. I better go inside and get Grandpa his breakfast. You kids have fun at school." She shooed me into the car and waved as we drove away.

I kept looking back at Lynn as I drove us to school. Something about her was different. She seemed distracted when I asked her if she thought mom was losing her mind. Something I thought she would have at least chuckled at. Besides being preoccupied, there was something else.

"Are you wearing lipstick?" I asked suddenly, realizing what was different about her. I craned my neck to get a better look at her face.

"Watch the road!" she yelled. "You're going to get us killed."

"You are!" I laughed. "You're wearing make-up."

"Stop it!" she said, trying to keep a defensive tone, but a giggle escaped her closed mouth making a snorting sound, which made her laugh even harder.

"Look at my little sister, all grown up." I wiped a fake tear from my eye.

Lynn rolled her eyes playfully, and then her face became serious. "Do I look okay?" she asked. "Is my outfit cute? And my hair ... does my hair look fine?"

I pulled into a parking space in front of our school, put the car in park and looked over at my sister. She really did look different, drastically different, good different. She wasn't wearing too much make-up; just enough to bring out her beautiful big blue eyes. When she was younger, I would call her "bug eyes" because her eyes were so large, but now they were her best feature. Thankfully, with all the embellishments, she still looked her age.

"You're forgetting that I am your brother, who has no idea about girls' outfits or how to curl hair. Just please don't ever get contacts," I said shaking my head, "or I will be getting into plenty more fights like yesterday, but for an entirely different reason."

Lynn looked at me and smiled shyly. "Really?" she asked in a dreamy voice. She had taken her glasses off and pulled the visor down, to look at herself in the mirror. "So you did get into a fight," she said in the same dreamy voice.

I started to smile and wanted to tell her some of the details on how I had tried to avenge her, but her reflection had her undivided attention. “So when did you get the new clothes?” I asked instead, moving my hand up and down gesturing to her new wardrobe.

“Mom took me yesterday during your game,” she gushed. “Oh, by the way how did you do?”

“Well …,” I began, scratching the back of my head.

“Hey! I’ve got to go. My friend is waiting for me.” Lynn opened the door, “I will tell you about my shopping trip later.”

I had never seen Lynn this distracted before. It was kind of refreshing to witness. I followed after her. “Did you remember to lock your door?” I asked, like I do every morning. My iPod and laptop had been stolen from my car the year before, and since then I have made it a habit to lock my doors, even when I wasn’t leaving anything behind. Unfortunately I had to manually lock each door. A new vehicle with electric amenities was on the top of my wish list.

“Oops, I forgot.” Lynn ran back to the car.

“Hope you don’t lose your head today,” I teased.

I walked Lynn to her locker, mainly because I was still uneasy leaving her alone. After she had grabbed her binder and some books, she practically demanded I go to class. She rambled on about how I was hovering too much and how her friend would be there any minute. I gave in and settled for giving her a big bear hug. I laughed when she told me I was embarrassing her.

My mood dropped as soon as I walked into class. The consequences of the night before were weighing me down. It felt like a black storm was following me, Lynn had provided me with some sunshine but now I was entering the eye of the storm.

“Jared! My man!” said Derek. He was sitting in his chair looking over Kim who was perched on his desk. “I was waiting to talk to you after the game,” he said. “Where did you run off to?” Payton barely glanced at me as I walked toward her then went back to reading through her Psychology book.

Kim winked at me as I slumped into my chair, “He was occupied with something,” she said with a smile. I wondered if Payton could see the hairs on the back of my neck bristle.

“Or someone!” Derek said slapping my back. “It’s a good thing I didn’t find you then.”

"It sure was," said Kim. She had slipped off Derek's desk and rubbed my shoulder as she went to sit in her seat. "Could you imagine how embarrassing that would have been for you?"

I slid Kim's hand off my shoulder.

"Not really," answered Derek, oblivious to Kim's implications. "I've seen you two together plenty of times."

"Could we please talk about something else," I said through clenched teeth.

Mrs. Flint had started class and was busy writing on the board.

"Let's talk about how in just three days you will be experiencing one of the sickest parties of your life!"

"I doubt that," I whispered.

"You're still going, right?" Kim said to me.

"Of course he is! Without my boy, there *is* no party," said Derek, a little too loudly.

"Excuse me?" asked Mrs. Flint. She had stopped writing and was looking right at us. "Does one of you have something to add?" Mrs. Flint's eyes peered over the brim of her glasses. She really thought we had been talking about the material she was teaching.

I began shaking my head, when Payton spoke up. "I do," she said firmly. I resisted the urge to turn around. She cleared her throat and stated matter-of-factly, "In our book, I read that negative consequences will eventually affect those people who are involved in that kind of destructive behavior."

"That is correct," said Mrs. Flint. "However, those very consequences can, in turn, push that individual into the contemplation stage." Mrs. Flint went on to explain that, just like it sounds, a person in the contemplation stage begins to consider changing their negative, addictive behavior. And that that individual is more apt to accept information about how their behavior is damaging themselves and others.

"May I interrupt?" asked Payton. Once again I resisted the impulse to turn around, I wanted to see her face, see if she was intending to describe *my* behavior, just in a vague, round-about way. But I was kidding myself. I really didn't need to see her reaction to know that she intended for me, specifically, to hear everything she said.

"Certainly," Mrs. Flint beamed. "I love this interaction and participation. Let's all take a lesson from Ms. Carleton and voice our opinions and questions." Mrs. Flint opened her arms wide, suggesting that she was referring to the entire class.

"Thank you," Payton said politely.

"Here it comes," I thought.

"But isn't it true that someone could be stuck in the contemplation stage for years and that they may even move backward to the pre-contemplation stage?" Payton asked.

"Yes, you are correct again," said Mrs. Flint, "but you are forgetting the most important part, because contemplators can be helped into the next stage by non-judgmental information givers and also by people who encourage change. And the contemplation stage will end when the decision to change the negative behavior is ultimately made. Sometimes they may just need a little push from a true friend."

"Or a rough shove from an annoyed classmate," Payton said under her breath.

I felt so exposed, like I was an exhibit in a museum, encased in glass lying vulnerable for everyone to see. I didn't like feeling defenseless, which made me resent Payton for displaying my imperfections. The problem was I wasn't exposed to anyone else but myself.

So why did I feel so insecure?

"What happens after the contemplation stage ends?" asked the girl who sat in front of Derek.

Derek sighed loudly. "Who cares," he mumbled.

Mrs. Flint glared at Derek before smiling at the girl. "Those contemplators start preparing to take action because their pros for changing start to outweigh their cons," she answered.

"You got her started," Derek whispered to the girl. "Now she'll never stop."

"And the action stage will come next. It is when the change is actually being made. It is also the stage where there are the greatest chances for relapse. This is when the person needs to work hard on maintaining their change."

"Told you," Derek grumbled.

"Does anyone else want to add something before we move on?" Mrs. Flint grinned.

The room fell silent as Derek silently threatened anyone who dared to speak.

I tried to sleep when Mrs. Flint put on a documentary about addictive behaviors. Instead I ended up faking it while listening to my life's story played out for everyone to see. I listened to the five most common teenage addictions described in depth; Alcohol, smoking, drugs, videogames, and social media. Alcohol was number one. I learned that some people are prone to addiction when it comes to alcohol and some aren't. It all depends on who carries a genetic risk for it and apparently seventeen percent of the American population does. I didn't need to be tested to know that I made up a part of that percentage.

"It may be difficult to admit if you have any of these specific addictive behaviors," Mrs. Flint said after the video was done playing, "however, those who entertain these negative behaviors are the ones who need immediate change."

I felt sick.

"What if we don't have any of those addictive behaviors that were mentioned in the documentary?" asked the girl who sat in front of Derek. She probably felt it was safe to speak since Derek was snoring loudly behind her.

"There is always something that a person can change about themselves," Mrs. Flint added. "So keep thinking about what that *thing* is!"

By lunch I didn't feel much better, Payton had ignored me the entire class. It didn't help that I made no attempt to start a conversation. I had no idea what to say, and was pretty worried she would slap me, or worse, ignore me. I thought about skipping lunch and just going home early, however my mom's new occupation of being a stay-at-home mom made it hard to pull that off. Luckily I only had three more classes to endure and was on strict orders from Coach to skip practice and rest my arm the rest of the week so that I would be ready to play that next Tuesday.

"Lunch today just seems so boring after what happened yesterday," Gus laughed. "Where's my entertainment? I was hoping for a dinner and a show."

"Coach will probably imprison us to a lifetime of servitude if we get into trouble again," said Derek. He shook his head and muttered, "I'm actually scared of that man."

We all laughed because he was serious.

It felt like weeks since my fight. Yesterday had been such a long day and today wasn't looking any better. Ironically the only bright moment of the day was solely because of Lynn. I searched for her, scanning the large room unsuccessfully. The table she had been trapped at yesterday was empty. Thankfully, I wasn't so worried about her anymore, mainly because I knew she wasn't alone and it seemed that she had actually found a genuine friend who enjoyed her company.

"I've invited the whole cheerleading team to your party Derek," said Kim, "I hope you don't mind." She smiled.

"If by 'don't mind' you mean, ecstatic? Then I don't mind at all!" Derek laughed. "This weekend is going to be memorable." He leaned back in his chair and put his feet up on the lunch table right next to my cheeseburger.

Disgusted I walked to throw the rest of my lunch away just as Payton walked past me, heading toward the far doors. She looked nervous so I stepped out of her way. I wanted to say something, but felt keeping my mouth shut was the best option. My dad would always call me the "king of justification," I didn't mind how he viewed me but I didn't want to be dubbed that title by Payton. Just before I could throw my lunch away, Payton came running from behind and cut in between me and the trash can. I must of had a shocked look on my face, because she briefly smiled, then put a folded piece of paper on top of my cheeseburger. She walked away, never looking back. I, on the other hand, watched her leave and kept watching even after she'd left my sight.

Six

I wish I could have dissected the sentence, maybe found some hidden message behind the obvious. I used to get notes in elementary school all the time. The girl who would sit next to me would send her friend with a note. My name would be written on top. Those notes were loaded with double meanings. This one wasn't. Before walking into class I unfolded and reread Payton's note from the day before. Her neat cursive said no more than, *"The person will compulsively engage in the negative behavior over and over even if he or she doesn't want to."*

It was a simple non-judgmental fact.

"What's that?" Kim asked from behind me.

I jumped and then frantically shoved the paper into my pocket, "It's nothing," I said without turning and then quickly walked to my seat.

Throughout the second half of first period we worked silently on our chapter reviews. I was finishing up my "Stages of Change" crossword puzzle when Kim leaned over to me and whispered, "Is two down preparation, or action?" I read the hint, "Individuals in this stage plan on changing their negative behavior and to take action within the next month."

"Preparation," I answered quietly, still staring at my paper.

The next month?

I knew I had certain bad habits I needed to change. I was doing things I didn't necessarily like to do, but I didn't know if I were ready to lose it all. Lose it all for the possibility that Payton may glance in my direction, that is, if I hadn't already burned that bridge.

Payton had finished her work as I stared blankly at my paper. I could hear her putting her stuff away. It dawned on me that I hadn't looked at her once the entire class. I had walked into the room with my head down, her note burning a hole in my pocket, and hadn't interacted with her in any way and wasn't planning on it anytime soon. She seemed perfectly content imagining me not there.

"Two more days," Derek said while leaning over his desk to punch my shoulder. "It looks like you can use some of what I'll be serving on Saturday."

"Tell me about it," I mumbled, without turning around. I wanted to obstruct my guilty face from the only person's opinion I cared about at the moment. I shouldn't have said anything.

Derek slid from his desk and crouched next to mine. "My parents left for their cruise on Monday," he said. He pulled a Snickers bar from his pocket and tore off the wrapper. "I am so lucky they didn't find out about this party and send my aunt to stay with me like last time." He took a large bite. Long strands of caramel hung from his lips, sticking to the bottom of his square chin.

"Gross!" said Kim.

"What?" asked Derek laughing, "I'm saving some for later."

"Mr. Dixon!"

We all looked up. Mrs. Flint was standing in front of the aisle. Her frail hands were on her bony hips. "Have you finished your review, young man?"

"Yes, ma'am," he answered with a wide grin.

"Very good, but I must ask you to go back to your seat so the others around you may finish as well. And please save your chocolate bar for lunch."

"All right," Derek said, waiting for her to walk away before shoving the rest of his Snickers into his mouth. "I hope you're ready to get wasted," Derek said with his mouth full, making him sound like a three year old, which made his statement sound that much more inappropriate.

I had no comment. I didn't necessarily feel ready but knew that it didn't make a difference. Thankfully Derek decided to sleep for the last ten minutes of class, since his enthusiasm regarding this weekend was making the silence between Payton and me unbearable. I wondered if she were expecting me to say something about her note. If so, I had no clue what to say. The tension was driving me nuts. Unable to bear it a minute longer, I turned to my left and sat sideways in my chair with my back facing Kim. I didn't want her to overhear our conversation.

I bent down to tie my shoe that didn't need to be tied, trying to muster some courage but feeling like a complete idiot. She was just a girl; why was I so scared of her? I cleared my throat and could feel my face go red. "I, uh…read your note."

There was a short pause and then Payton said sharply, "What?"

I wasn't expecting that reply.

Shocked I looked over at her. She was glowing! Her blonde hair was curled and hung over her shoulders and her bright yellow shirt and white skirt were blinding. The only contrast to her shining appearance was her face. Her beautiful eyes narrowed and her lips tightened.

"Who in their right mind would read a note given to them? I never read notes that are given to me." Payton's efforts to keep a stern face were failing her, the dimple in her left cheek was showing as she tried to keep composure, which made her look so cute. I could tell it made her feel good to make fun of me, and I couldn't blame her for it. She raised her eyebrows and gave me a look like, "Duh!"

The conversation seemed over before it ever began. Feeling dejected, I turned back around. I wasn't sure how I had expected her to react, but I did know it was my fault. My own indecision was giving me whiplash, and it was hard convincing someone to join the ride. Psychology was almost over and I couldn't believe that my easiest class was becoming the hardest to go to. I quickly finished my review, shoved my book into my backpack then watched painfully as the second hand on the clock hanging on the wall moved slowly around.

I jumped when the bell rang, I must have drifted off. I slowly grabbed my backpack feeling a little disoriented as Payton raced past me and out the door.

"Wake up!" I said kicking Derek's chair. His arms that had been folded against his chest flung forward as he smacked both hands loudly on the top of his desk.

"You scared me half to death!" he yelled, then ran to catch up to me as I left the room. We walked in silence toward the lockers when Derek stopped me, "What's your deal?" he asked.

"What do you mean?" I mumbled then started walking to the school's west building.

"You've been acting like a chick."

I stopped. I could feel my face getting hot, "What did you just call me?"

"You've just been acting moody lately, that's all," Derek said quickly. "Forget I said anything."

I felt guilty for letting what Derek said get to me. He had hit the nail right on the head, I did feel different. Maybe that was why I got so upset. "I must just need some more sleep," I paused, "sorry for jumping on you like that."

"No problem," said Derek. His lax personality made my apology easy. "Well, then it is a good thing Coach banned you from practice tonight."

"My arm seems fine." I rotated it back and forth. "I hate missing practice. Last night my arm still felt stiff, so missing yesterday's practice didn't bother me so much, but I feel completely healed today," I said. I dreaded missing those next two practices. It didn't feel right; it felt unnatural.

"If I were you, I would take advantage of the break," Derek said. "You could also catch up on that sleep you so desperately need."

I smirked. We were getting closer to my locker and I was about to apologize again for my hot headedness when Derek awkwardly stopped. My heart started beating faster. I waited a second to look up, preparing myself for a repeat of Monday. This time I wasn't going to let a stranger think he had intimidated me in any way, and I sure as heck wasn't going to back down. When I looked up my heart beat even faster, but for a much different reason. Payton was standing by my locker waiting for me.

"Derek, I'll uh, talk to you later," I said, giving him a nod.

"Sure," he said slowly, raising and lowering his eyebrows a few times, while smiling widely.

I was kidding myself if I thought I could hide my feelings for Payton from Derek. He, along with everyone in my psychology class including Kim, had a pretty good idea of my infatuation.

Once Derek had left, I slowly walked to my locker. I felt some comfort noticing that Payton kept playing with her hair, a nervous habit of hers that I had grown fond of. She handed me a folded pink paper, then stood there twisting her hair in her finger.

I looked at the paper in my hand and said, "Thanks."

She backed away a few steps so that I could reach my locker. Then looked down at her shoes and said quickly, "I need to get to class." I knew there was more she had wanted to say. Conversation used to be so effortless with us; now there was obvious strain. I waited until she was out of sight before reading what she had written. *"It's easy to follow the crowd, but even easier to get lost in it."*

ꝏ

"Jared! Time for dinner," yelled Lynn.

I was busy sulking. Instead of being on the field pitching the baseball, I was getting ready to have dinner with my family, my whole family, which was strange. I couldn't remember the last time we had sat down and had a real meal together with everyone. Lynn had orchestrated the entire thing and was persistent that everyone would participate, but I wasn't in the mood to fake being a normal family.

"Jared!" Lynn yelled louder. I could hear her footsteps crossing the wood floor as she walked to my room.

I groaned, and then rolled off my bed. I had been so comfortable in my dark room, wallowing in self pity. Payton's pink paper was lying on the ground where I had left it. It was the real reason I had wasted the last four hours moping in silence. I wasn't sure what to think of it, so instead I didn't think about anything. I pulled out her first note from my pocket and grabbed the pink paper off the floor shoving them quickly under my mattress just as Lynn flung my door open.

"The food is getting cold," she pleaded.

I took a deep breath and slowly exhaled, trying not to lose my cool. Lynn understood immediately. "Oops, sorry," she whispered then slowly backed out of my room, gently shutting the door. A second later I heard a light tap.

"Come in," I said calmly, the breather had helped my attitude.

Lynn popped her head in, smiled, and then said, "Dinner's ready."

"Thank you," I said.

"I made it!" she beamed.

"In that case, go ahead without me," I said grabbing my stomach as I walked out into the hall.

"I bet it's better than anything you could make," she said, pushing me playfully into the wall as we walked to the kitchen.

My dad was sitting at the head of the dining room table talking on his cell phone and didn't look up when I came into the room. "I needed you to have made that appointment a week ago! What am I paying you for?" he yelled. When my mom came in with a basket of rolls and Lynn with a casserole dish overflowing with white sauce, he held up his finger and briskly left the room. I could hear him arguing about how much money losing this client could potentially cost him.

The three of us sat, waiting.

Five minutes later my dad came into the room looking on edge. Mom quickly started dishing everyone's plates. "Lynn worked really hard on this meal," she said, smiling admiringly at Lynn.

"Mom helped, too." Lynn blushed.

My dad started digging in. He took a large bite of the noodles, chewed slowly, and then swallowed. Lynn was staring at him from the corner of her eye. "This is delicious," he said, smiling slightly. Lynn couldn't have looked more pleased. And I had to admit, it didn't taste half bad.

We ate most of our meal in silence. My mom finally spoke up asking my dad how his trip to California went. Judging from their awkwardness I could tell they probably hadn't talked since their fight on Monday. My dad mumbled about how he didn't accomplish everything he had wanted while he was down there and needed to go back next weekend to finish up some loose ends.

"Couldn't you go another weekend?" my mom asked, her eyebrows pulled together causing worry lines to crease her forehead. I knew what she was getting at and didn't like it.

"You never told me how your shopping trip went with mom," I said to Lynn, in an effort to derail the conversation.

"Oh, we had so much fun!" Lynn squealed. She started telling me about all of the stores that they went to and which items of clothing or accessories she had gotten from each store. Unfortunately the other conversation stayed right on track. I faked interest toward Lynn's story as I intently listened to my parents. Lynn was too excited to realize what I was doing.

"I've already made arrangements to go that weekend. Did you have plans or something?" he asked sounding exhausted and irritable.

"I thought we could do something special as a family, you know for ... Jared's birthday," she whispered, trying to keep her voice low. She knew as well as I, that he had forgotten.

"Oh," my dad said. He rubbed his forehead and said something about having a headache. My mom ran to the kitchen and came back with two pills. "Kate, I just can't reschedule this trip. You guys could still do something, I don't need to be here, right?" he said quietly.

My mom quickly glanced in my direction.

"That sounds awesome," I interrupted Lynn, trying to make it appear like I had been enveloped in her the entire time.

My mom answered with a quiet, "Right."

I didn't need anyone around for my birthday, especially my dad. I hated the idea of my mom planning anything, and I really didn't want this to cause another conflict. We all seemed to be managing this uncomfortable meal fine without bringing up incidents that had happened the last time we were all together.

Lynn turned her attention to our dad and started to recount her entire shopping trip again. My mom started to fill an extra plate with the casserole, a roll and lots of green beans.

"Where's Grandpa'?" I asked, feeling a little guilty that I hadn't noticed earlier.

"He hasn't been feeling very well. Earlier today he had a fever and has been sleeping most of the afternoon. Once he woke up, he insisted on watching television while he ate." She handed me the plate. "Will you take this down to him?"

I carried the dish to the basement and found him sitting in his recliner watching the news.

"Can you believe it? The worlds gone crazy," he said as soon as I entered his bedroom.

I nodded then said, "You've been eating down here a lot this week?"

"Where do I usually eat?" he asked, not being sarcastic at all, he was genuinely unsure of the answer.

"Usually you eat upstairs," I answered.

"I do?" he asked softly.

"Don't worry about it, Gramps'," I said, as I set up his collapsible dinner tray next to him and placed the remote on it.

"I hear you have been feeling sick," I said. "What do you think is wrong?"

"I'm old," he answered.

I laughed and then said, "You look plenty young to me, Grandpa. Mom says that she will be down in just a minute to see if you need anything." I left the room keeping his door open.

When I came back upstairs Lynn was still talking excitedly to my dad. She was sitting in the chair next to him and could barely keep her body still. "Please Dad? Please?" she begged.

My mom looked just as excited and anxious to hear his answer. However she couldn't wait, she interjected quickly. "We've already been talking about it, and we have a great meal planned."

"It will be just like tonight," Lynn squealed. "This was kind of my practice run."

"I don't see why I have to be present," my dad spoke slowly, looking from my mom back to Lynn. "I was going to go golfing with Bill."

I sat back in my chair and hoped to finish the rest of my meal in peace, but before I could even take a bite Lynn had turned to me, her face had dimmed slightly. He had deflated her. When he messed with me I dealt with it, but Lynn didn't deserve to be ignored. "You will be here Jared, right?"

I looked around the table, my mom was staring at me intently and my dad seemed relieved to have someone else in the hot seat. "Be here for what?" I asked cautiously.

"For dinner on Saturday," she answered. I was confused, why were dinners becoming such a big deal in our family?

"I...uh, don't know. I kind of have this thing with some friends," I said slowly and then gave a weak smile. I could see my mom's instant concern when I mentioned doing things with friends and my dad's jaw-line tighten.

"What exactly are you going to be doing with friends?" asked my dad, getting straight to the point. My parents had never caught me drinking, but they had their suspicions.

"Some of us from the baseball team were going to go to the park to throw some balls, since I'm missing most of the practices this week." I knew this would get his attention. I just needed him to focus on something besides what I was actually going to be doing that weekend.

"You've been missing practices? Why?" he asked sternly.

"During my game on Tuesday I messed my arm up a little, Coach wanted me to rest it these last few days," I said.

"Hmm," my dad calmed down a little. It was working. "Just be careful, throw a few pitches to loosen it up, but don't go all out. All you need is to ruin your future because you were showing off for some friends."

"So I can go?"

My dad just nodded. Lynn looked close to tears.

My mom wrapped her arms protectively around her and announced, "Lynn has been planning this dinner all week." My mom would never come out and demand us to be there, at least not my dad, but I could tell she was boiling inside. I looked over at Lynn and felt guilty.

I sighed. "What time will dinner be at?" I asked.

Lynn jumped off of my mom's lap and ran around the table to give me a hug. "Thank you, Thank you, so much," she said.

"Wait a second!" I said laughing. "I haven't agreed to anything. I can come to dinner, but I can't stay for long."

"That's fine," Lynn said, hugging me again. "He will be here at five!"

"Who?" I asked, once again, confused.

"B.J., the friend I have been telling you about. He is coming to dinner."

"What?" I said, laughing out loud. "Your friend's a guy?" Suddenly things seemed to make more sense. Lynn's behavior and sudden changes in appearance were solely to impress her new "friend."

My dad looked at my mom, and then asked, "You knew about this?"

She smiled at Lynn. "I've been helping her plan it."

"Is this a boyfriend?" my dad asked; his posture stiffened as he said the last word.

Lynn's face instantly flushed, she looked down and said loudly, "Dad! We're just friends." Her reaction was evidence enough that she wouldn't have minded introducing him as such.

"What is so special about this boy that you need to make a big production?" My dad seemed to relax a little, even though I am pretty sure he could tell, as well as I, that Lynn had strong feelings for this person.

"He is tutoring me in math, and always asks about my family, I thought it would be nice to invite him over."

"And we all need to be here for this?" my dad said, not requiring an answer. He paused a few seconds then added, "I will talk to Bill and see if he can push golfing to Sunday."

Lynn just nodded as a giant smile escaped her lips. "He is so excited to finally meet you!" She stared right at me as she said this.

It struck me as odd, hadn't she just met him, and why would this guy care to meet me at all. Unable to let it slide I asked defensively, "Why does he want to meet me?"

She shrugged then added, "He wants to meet everybody."

My mind was trying to replay the events of what happened two days ago in the lunch room. I didn't notice anyone else around Lynn besides those five guys, which made me feel extremely uneasy about the entire thing.

Seven

I tried to spend most of my Saturday relaxing and playing video games but I had been receiving texts from Derek all day long. I think he was worried I was going to end up not showing, and I'm pretty sure he was planning on me making a fool of myself, once again. Lynn and my mom had been cooking all afternoon, the dining table was already set and Grandpa was asleep on the living room sofa. I hadn't seen my dad all day. He probably completely forgot about trying to make it tonight or didn't care. I had other things I would have rather been doing, too, but was doing this for Lynn.

"Will you make sure the family room floor doesn't need to be vacuumed, sweetie," my mom said rubbing my arm as soon as I walked into the kitchen. She seemed just as excited as Lynn, if not more.

"Sure," I answered, and then grabbed a handful of cherry tomatoes sitting in a bowl on the counter. Ever since I could remember I loved eating cherry tomatoes. When I was young, my dad used to take me to the market and buy me a bag. He hated them, but he always wanted to buy them for me.

"Hey, those are for the salad," Lynn whined, shoving me with both hands out of the kitchen.

I quickly popped the rest of the tomatoes into my mouth but one. "For your salad," I said handing her the tomato. She ripped it from my hand and stormed back to the counter.

"I don't know why you like them so much; they are nasty," she said pulling a face.

I was getting ready to check the family room floor when the doorbell rang. My mom and Lynn froze. They stared at each other with horrified looks on their faces. "He's early," Lynn whispered. "The food isn't ready yet!"

I just laughed at both of them; they were acting ridiculous. "You would think we are having a celebrity over for dinner."

"Shhh," my mom said smiling. "Just go answer the door and entertain him while we take care of the finishing touches."

I shouldn't have laughed, and I should have been hiding out in my room. Now I had the unpleasant chore of having an unwanted conversation with a complete stranger. My mom pointed toward the entryway and said, "Hurry!"

I opened the front door just as the doorbell rang again. My plan was to have him sit in the living room next to the dining room table and leave him there; however, once I saw him, my plan changed. I didn't even want him in my home, so I left him standing in the doorway.

I paced back and forth, ignoring the uncomfortable tingling I was getting up my arms and legs. There he was again. He was even wearing the same white sweater, causing a bad case of déjà vu. Was this joker serious? He didn't say anything, just watched as I tried to get control of myself.

My mom must have been worried when she didn't hear anything, because she came rushing around the corner. She gave me a warning glance as she walked past me to invite our guest in. Lynn was right behind my mom but was too excited to see her visitor to recognize any tension in the room. She jumped up and down when she saw him then blushed when she spotted what he was carrying.

It wasn't until then that I noticed a bouquet of purple carnations in his left hand. Lynn grabbed his right arm and led him into the living room, eyeing the flowers the entire time. He looked around the room from person to person. I scowled when he glanced at me, but his expression never changed. He kept smiling as he looked at me, then at my mom, then back at me again.

"This is B.J. everybody," Lynn said, her face beaming. "And this is my mom Kate and my brother Jared." She pointed to both of us. I glared. "And my grandpa is in the other room."

"Mrs. Anderson ... these are for you," he said handing my mom the carnations. Lynn's face fell. My mom didn't notice Lynn's disappointment because she was in complete shock as she took the bouquet.

This guy was getting on my nerves.

My mom had fallen for this guy just as fast as Lynn had. She held the flowers up to her nose then touched a petal softly. B.J. watched her intently. My mom didn't say anything; she just smiled and then left the room. Lynn looked like she had recovered from her disappointment. She turned to me and said, "B.J. has been waiting to meet you."

"Why were you at my locker the other day?" I asked. My voice shook as I tried to keep from yelling.

"To meet you," he answered matter-of-factly. I felt like I was being mocked, but didn't have much reason to lash out, yet. I realized that I had no desire for him or Lynn to have any kind of relationship, and the fact that his intentions seemed unclear, made me angrier.

I turned to Lynn, in an effort to not scream at B.J. and asked, "Where did you meet this guy?"

Lynn clearly didn't like my tone, because she answered defensively, "He was the only one helping me when those losers at school surrounded me."

That hurt.

She knew what I had done for her that day, we had made eye contact. Now I was receiving no credit for it. Lynn looked away from me while biting her lip. I could tell she felt guilty and regretted losing her temper. I didn't know how to react; I guess I was right in thinking this guy had been there that afternoon. I realized that instead of being one of the bullies, *he* was the hero, and not me. I had barely come to grips with his role in helping my sister when the timeline in my head started flashing red warning signals. I had ended up fighting those losers the day after he had shown up at my locker. I felt confused and defensive.

Was this kid trying to meet me before he ever met Lynn?

I wasn't sure how to approach the subject and missed my chance. B.J. backed away and started looking at our family pictures on the wall. Both Lynn and I watched him. He paused at a picture of us in the Bahamas three years ago; we were on the beach. He went to touch the glass but stopped. Lynn looked at me with an awkward smile, and then shrugged. "Um, B.J. would you like to sit down while dinner finishes cooking?" she asked. "It should only be about ten more minutes."

B.J. stayed by our wall of pictures. He slowly looked from one picture to the next. My mom had a habit of taking a lot of pictures and instead of replacing the older ones with new ones, she just kept adding to our wall. Unfortunately for me, that meant I got to relive my awkward preteen years on a daily basis.

"Your family has a lot of pictures," he said, mirroring my thoughts exactly. He backed a few steps from the wall like he was trying to take it all in at once, and then held his hands up to his face, looking like he was taking a mental picture of our "picture wall."

I was really starting to believe this guy was some deranged stalker. My mom came back in with a vase filled with the carnations he had given her. She smiled and announced, "Dinner will be ready in just five minutes." Her eyes were red and a little swollen. I thought it odd that she was so emotional over flowers. "Jared, will you bring Grandpa to the table?" she asked.

Before I could even nod, B.J. piped up, "I'll help!" I left the room not waiting to see if he would follow, but hoping he wouldn't. I grabbed the wheelchair from behind the living room sofa. Grandpa was asleep. "Do you want me to hold the wheelchair while you put him in it?" B.J. asked from behind me.

I didn't answer.

Instead I walked in front of my grandpa and gently woke him. He slept almost all the time. Some days it was hard to keep him awake for longer than twenty minutes at a time, but other days he was as sharp as a tack. On those days his personality would shine through and I got to see how he used to be before the disease had taken over. He looked at me confused and I could tell it was going to be one of those not so sharp days.

"Hey, Gramps'," I said.

"Who in the blazes are you?"

"I'm your grandson."

"What? I'm too young to have grandchildren!" he exclaimed. I smiled.

My grandpa rubbed his head looking confused and then said, "My wife is going to kill me when she finds out."

I had almost forgotten that B.J. was in the room with me; that was until he laughed out loud. He laughed so hard that his eyes started watering. I couldn't tell if it were all an act, or if he genuinely thought the comment was *that* hysterical. Either way he ruined the moment for me.

B.J. gained some composure and rolled the wheelchair over next to me. I wrapped my arms around my grandpa, just below his armpits and lifted him off the sofa. His legs weren't completely useless, because he helped keep balance as I lowered him onto his wheelchair.

B.J. walked around until he was in front of my grandpa and bent down until he was eye level with him. He smiled and then asked, "How are you?"

My grandpa's eyes lit up. He grabbed B.J.'s hands, squeezing them with his frail fingers. "How are you my boy?"

"I'm doing well," he answered, "just getting ready to have dinner with your family."

"I've missed you grandson," he said patting B.J. on the arm. B.J. just smiled. I was not okay with this. My grandpa thought B.J. was me and this kid went along with it!

"Is it all right if I push you into the dining room?" B.J. asked.

"Of course."

I rolled my eyes at B.J., wanting him to notice. Instead he walked past me smiling as he pushed the wheelchair. "Are you coming?" he called over his shoulder before he left the room.

I had to hold my breath and count to ten. Unfortunately I still didn't feel better, so I did it again. I could hear my mom and Lynn gushing over how helpful B.J. was being and how good he was with Grandpa. I then decided that I had had enough of this charade, you can only fake it for so long before it ends up driving you nuts. And apparently I was only capable of barely faking it for merely ten minutes. I stalked back into the dining room.

"I think I am going to just head on out," I declared.

"No! You're not," said my dad.

We all turned toward the front door. My dad must have snuck in quietly without being noticed. He was wearing a dark blue polo shirt and khaki shorts. He must have gone golfing after all. "Lynn has worked hard to put this family dinner together, so the entire family will attend." He looked sternly into my eyes, waiting for a confrontation.

"I'm still leaving in an hour. Since punctuality is not a necessity, staying the entire evening shouldn't be one either," I said seething with sarcasm.

My dad walked over to the table and then in an answer to my obvious disrespect, said, "Well it looks like the party will liven up in an hour then." My mom laughed uncomfortably and then introduced my dad to B.J. "Nice to meet you," he said briskly.

"Very nice to meet you, Mr. Anderson, sir," B.J. acted unaffected by my dad's unfriendliness.

"Um, Michael's fine." I could tell that my dad also felt uneasy around B.J. The entire meal he kept looking at him out of the corner of his eye and shifting awkwardly in his chair. He didn't ask too many questions during dinner and I obviously didn't say a word to anyone. I still felt that weird electric feeling when B.J. was near, but was starting to get used to it, and wondered if my dad was feeling something similar. Lynn and my mom must have been the only ones not experiencing the uncomfortable tingling because they carried on like nothing was wrong. In fact they acted like everything B.J. said was captivating.

"So where do you live?" my mom asked, after B.J. had finished explaining how Lynn and he had met. He left out the fight completely, which was the only thing I was grateful for when it came to B.J. and this evening. He had only told them that Lynn had looked like she needed a friend.

"I live with my grandma, an uncle, and two great grandparents," he answered.

"Oh! Well, that explains why you are so good with my dad," she beamed. "How long have you lived with them, if you don't mind me asking?" my mom pried.

"I've lived with them ever since I was a baby. They have done a great job taking care of me."

I could tell that my mom wanted to ask more questions about his family but thought better of it. "So did you just move here?" she asked instead.

"No, he has been homeschooled," Lynn answered for him. "This is his first year in public school."

"Wow, this must be a big adjustment for you. What made you decide to go to public school?" my mom asked.

"I just felt like it was where I needed to be."

"Well, we are glad you decided to," my mom smiled. "Aren't we?" she looked at both my dad and me. I was shocked she had taken the risk in hoping we would answer congenially. I in fact didn't acknowledge that I had been spoken to, and my dad grunted as he conveniently shoveled a spoonful of potatoes into his mouth.

My grandpa who had been slowly eating some cooked corn looked at B.J. sitting next to him, shook his head in disbelief and then chuckled. He pointed a bony finger at him and said, "You are a tricky young man!"

B.J. gave him a mischievous grin as my mom whispered from across the table, "My dad has dementia, so don't take much of what he has to say literally." Grandpa slipped back into his own little world, unaware that anyone was sharing a conversation about him. Lynn giggled watching him struggle with a kernel of corn. Every time he would move his fork to his mouth his unsteady hands would cause it to fall off.

"Oh? But this time Grandpa is telling the truth!" B.J. said. He leaned to his right where Lynn was sitting and whispered, "I am a very tricky person." Her giggle stopped short. She snapped her mouth shut and her cheeks turned red. It looked like B.J.'s close proximity was going to cause her to go into cardiac arrest. B.J. winked at her.

"Let me help you, Dad." My mom stood and walked over to my grandpa. She loaded up a forkful of corn and fed him a bite. "There," she said patting his hand, "now it's time for your medicine."

"My mom used to be a nurse," Lynn said to B.J. when my mom had come back into the dining room holding a small paper cup filled with all sorts of colorful pills. "She used to care for sick babies."

"Really?" B.J. seemed genuinely interested.

"I know CPR!" Lynn added, and then blushed at her outburst. "Well, mom wanted both Jared and me to be certified, just in case."

My mom patted Lynn on the arm and then said, "I used to work in the NICU at Sunrise Hospital in Henderson." She finished helping my grandpa take his last pill and then sat back in her seat.

"You don't anymore?"

My mom looked over at my dad who was sitting silently. He never looked up. "About fifteen years ago I decided to get my degree in nursing. I wanted to be able to help those tiny beautiful babies and help make their families' prayers come true." My mom stopped, lost in her thoughts, and then said, "I loved those babies. I loved my job."

"I bet you were really good at it," B.J. said.

"I'd like to think so," she said almost dreamily. "But I am a stay-at-home mom, for nearly six months, now." Her tone had changed. Even a stranger would have been able to sense the regret. We had lost her, even if it were only for a few seconds. She had been sucked back into the life of tiny fingers, miniature diapers, and beeping heart monitors.

We watched my mom in silence. My dad cleared his throat, but never said anything. No one was sure what to say. One thing I couldn't blame my dad for was aggressively persuading her to quit her job. She had been obsessed. As soon as Lynn started school, she had wanted to spend every waking hour at that hospital, far away from her life here. She would pick up extra shifts whenever she could. Most the time I would play parent to Lynn, so that our mom could live in a fake world filled with little babies—little babies just like the one she lost so many years ago. One night six months ago my dad had reached a breaking point after my mom had slipped into another one of her depressions after one of her preemies had lost his battle, "His lungs were just too underdeveloped," she had cried.

"Don't you see what you are doing to yourself?" my dad had pleaded with my mom. "It's like you want to keep reliving the pain over and over again." After that, Lynn and I didn't see my mom for over three days. My dad tried to help out around the house and with us, but we didn't need much; we were used to it. When she finally came out of it, she was different, she seemed better, and she never went back to work again.

B.J. reached across the table and gently touched my mom's hand, bringing her back to reality. "But I just love being able to spend more time here, with my two kids," she added. Lynn said something about loving having Mom around to go shopping with and everybody went back to eating their dinner.

"This food is really good, Lynn." B.J. broke the silence. "I bet your mom taught you how to cook so well."

"Yep!" Lynn answered grinning from ear to ear.

"I could use some more tomatoes on my salad though," B.J. said. Lynn quickly grabbed the salad bowl and thrust it toward him. "You should have some too," B.J. suggested pointing to Lynn's plate.

"Sure," she said, smiling as B.J. topped her salad with two ripe tomatoes.

Lynn's infatuation was nauseating. I was actually worried for her. B.J. was playing nice right now and I know Lynn was taking everything he said the wrong way, or I hoped she was. I just couldn't let myself believe that this kid had any real romantic interest in her. It did seem like he was treating her more like a little sister than something more, though. I could have been wrong, which meant I needed to protect her from being hurt and if that involved me chasing away the only friend she thought she had, so be it. I figured she would forgive me for it in the long run.

Dinner had gone longer than I had thought it would. I looked at the clock on my phone as I brought my dinner dish into the kitchen. Derek's party had already started. I sat my plate on the counter and walked past my mom who was playfully forcing our dinner guest out of the kitchen as he insisted on helping her with the dishes. My dad had just barely left, rambling on about how he needed to get to the office to run some numbers. I had laughed out loud at his hypocritical excuse and said, "Well it looks like the real party is getting underway a little earlier than planned!"

My dad looked too uncomfortable to comment or discipline. Our family knew that he was anti-social and wanted nothing more than to be by himself and right now, thanks to our visitor; that meant out of the house. B.J. had stood to shake my dad's hand before he left which I think both impressed and unnerved him. What fifteen year old kid would shake an adult's hand telling them it was nice to finally meet them?

"I'm leaving, too," I said to no one in particular as soon as my dad's car had pulled out of the driveway. "It's been a blast!" I said, smothering the last word with as much sarcasm as I could muster.

My mom's plastered on fake smile sealed the deal. I was going to be able to leave, no questions asked. I realized that to save herself any embarrassment, my mom would rather pretend that she trusted me wholeheartedly with any activity I may or may not have been participating in that night. “Um, sweetie,” my mom said right before I shut the door to leave, “remember who you are!”

Unfortunately that little comment had soiled my clean getaway. She had managed a “Hail Mary” of sorts, by getting in the last, guilt-laced, word. I was still going to do what I was planning on doing that night, now I just had to know that she had attempted to derail my runaway train, just like she always did.

Eight

Remember who I am?

It's not as easy as it sounds and would be simpler if I had an idea of who I was in the first place. My mom's comment had followed me as I drove the six blocks to Derek's house and kept pestering me as I sought out a way to drown my worries. The red plastic cup Derek offered me was a start. My problems were shoved deep inside of me as the clear burning liquid ran down my throat.

"I was worried you weren't coming." Derek said with a smile. He had two young looking girls, whom I think were freshmen, following him around. It was weird to think that they were the same age as Lynn. "Do you want a refill?" he asked looking down at my cup.

"Sure ... err, just bring me the whole bottle," I mumbled.

"Now that's what I'm talking about!" he cheered and then walked to the kitchen.

There were more people there than I had thought were going to be. I walked around a group of girls who were dancing to some music Derek had playing over his intercom system and sat on a sofa in the living room. The French doors leading out to the patio and pool were open and I could see at least twenty people swimming with even more trying to cram themselves into the Jacuzzi.

"Here you go; drink up!" Derek handed me a heavy glass bottle. "We are lucky Bobby's older brother was willing to buy us the alcohol."

"To Bobby's older brother," I said loudly as I raised the bottle into the air.

"To Bobby's older brother," a few voices rang out from the crowd.

I looked over at Derek who had his cup raised above his head. His hair was so long that it hung over his eyes and he wore a fitted buttoned collared shirt with jeans that were at least two sizes too small for him, making him look like he was a rancher on a Texas farm. Derek was known to be mildly eccentric at times but this getup took it to a whole new level. He was pulling out all the stops for this party.

"You look ridiculous," I said.

"Don't hate the player, hate the game," Derek said as he ran his hand dramatically through his hair. "I don't see these ladies complaining," he added and then grabbed each girl around the waist.

"You got me there," I said. "If only I could be so lucky."

The blonde to Derek's right brightened at my comment and said playfully, "Oh, but you can!"

Derek tightened his grasp.

"Girls, let's not forget, Jared isn't necessarily available." Kim had snuck up behind me. She wrapped her arms around my neck and gave me a kiss on the cheek as he held up a camera and took a picture. "Now that one's a keeper," she said and then pointed at the blonde, "It looks like you are stuck with Derek." I was excited to see her. I needed some companionship because I felt so completely alone.

"Watch it," Derek said. "Girls, how about we check out my pool?" he directed them toward the backyard and then turned back to me and whispered, "I'll catch you later. I need to get away while I still have them." He winked.

"It looks like we are going to have a little party of our own." Kim grabbed the bottle I was still holding.

"Getting totally hammered tonight doesn't sound like a bad idea," I said dully.

"Don't sound so excited," Kim whispered in my ear. She poured herself a cup and then refilled mine. We sat there talking for a while. More people showed up. A vase and a picture frame were broken when two juniors got into a fight, and my red cup kept getting refilled.

That night I wasn't in much of the mood to put on a show, much to Derek's disappointment and Kim's delight. I was content sitting on the same sofa where I had been for the past two hours. I also felt that if I tried to get up, I might not be able to walk and I'd fall right back down where I was. It was getting harder to carry on a coherent conversation, and I wasn't the only one.

"What's your deal?" Kim said loudly as she leaned over putting her full weight on me, her chin rested on my shoulder. She laughed randomly when I looked at her. I wasn't sure what she had meant. "No seriously," she said straightening up and pointing her finger at me. "Do you like Payton?" she asked slurring her words together.

It was hard to concentrate, but I knew well enough that this was a talk I didn't want to be having, even if Kim might not remember it clearly the next day, which was a good possibility. For every refill I had, Kim had had two. I could tell early on that she was anxious around me, and I had a feeling that her nervousness was due to what she had gotten the guts to just ask me.

I sat there quietly. We both sat quietly for a long time. "I have been watching you with her," she finally said, putting her cup down. This was a new side to Kim that I hadn't seen before. She looked down at her hands, which were tucked tightly in her lap. She seemed to be shrinking before me, any sign of confidence I had ever seen suddenly vanishing. I knew how she felt.

I still didn't say anything.

"I can try to be her, if that's what you want." She said this so quietly it was almost inaudible. I opened my mouth to object, when she quickly added, "But I am not sure if you do. The way you act around me, like tonight, makes me think that I am great for you and you for me."

"She doesn't want somebody like me," I mumbled, almost to myself.

Kim suddenly got angry, her voice rose, "What is it about her? I accept you for everything you are ... does she?" Kim looked at me intensely. "I just don't know why you would want to be around someone who, you are so sure, doesn't want you."

What she said made sense.

It would have been effortless to just tell Kim that she was right, that I had been wrong and that we could be together. I just wasn't sure how strongly I felt for her. "I do like you, Kim," I said cautiously. I knew I was treading on dangerous ground. "I enjoy the times that we spend together. I'm just not sure what I want exactly."

Kim looked genuinely hurt. She bit her lip as her eyes watered. "So I guess you'll just let me know then? That is, when you are sure of what you want."

"Yes, I will," was all I could say.

"Fine," Kim stood up abruptly and took a few seconds to get her footing. She then looked around awkwardly like she wanted to leave but wasn't sure where to go. "Um ... just remember, I won't be waiting forever." Her emotions took over; "I have some dignity," she said then let out a sob. She covered her mouth as she started to cry.

I felt horrible. I didn't want to hurt her, but at that moment I felt that if I said something that I didn't mean, but what she wanted to hear, I would cause more damage than good. I stood to try and comfort her. She backed away waving her hands frantically in front of her eyes, "Don't! I'm fine, I'm acting like such a baby," she said and then dabbed at the corner of her eyes with her fingers. "I'll see you at school on Monday." I didn't follow her as she walked away. I knew she wouldn't want me to.

I waited a few minutes before leaving. I didn't want to accidently run into her. I felt a little nauseous from the alcohol and was tired. I just wanted to go home and sleep. I found Derek in the front yard refereeing a boxing match between some kid and our team's right fielder, Rick. They were on a small patch of grass and several people were sitting on the decorative rocks laughing hysterically at the two of them trying to swing at each other's faces but missing horribly. I walked toward Derek, who had a whistle to his mouth getting ready to end the round when Rick tripped over himself and fell to the ground. Blood started gushing from his nose.

"I'm going to head out," I said. Derek looked at the watch on his wrist. "I know it's only ten, but I'm beat."

"Yea, I figured," Derek said with a sigh. "Kim's sister just came and picked her up."

"And?" I said, waiting for the rest of it.

"And ... she told me about your guys' talk." Derek handed his whistle to one of the girls standing next to him and told her to start the next match. "I get it," Derek said turning back to me. "Payton is gorgeous and ..."

"That's not the sole reason," I interrupted.

"And seems like an okay person," he said, acting like he wasn't so sure if it were true or not. "But Jared, Kim *is* a good person, who happens to be fighting for you."

It was seldom I got valuable advice from Derek, this was one time I took what he was saying seriously and put some thought into it. "I know," I said. The look on my face convinced him of my indecisiveness.

"You're confused?" It was more of an observation than a question. "People like Kim and me, we get you and we are your friends. You don't have to change to be with us," said Derek. He paused and scratched his head. "How much would you have to change to be with Payton?" he asked. "I just get the impression she wouldn't be caught dead at one of my parties."

I wasn't offended, because he was right. *How much would I have to change to even get a shot at asking Payton out?* I nodded to Derek in an attempt to acknowledge that I had heard what he was saying and was thinking about it. I walked down the driveway to the street. I felt sick. I really shouldn't have drunk as much as I did or even at all. I turned around and walked back to Derek, handing him my car keys. "I better walk the six blocks home. I'll be back in the morning to get my car."

ꕤ

"What are you doing?"

I nearly jumped ten feet into the air. I was so enveloped in my own thoughts that I hadn't seen the old red van slow down next to me as I walked down the road. Payton was looking out the passenger side window at me with a curious look on her face.

I dropped my head, baffled by the pure irony of the situation. Of all people, it had to be her. I was just three blocks from my house. I noticed a young blonde boy in the passenger seat. "Who's this?" I asked, dodging her question. I desperately didn't want to end up saying something I would regret later.

"He's my brother, Kevin," Payton answered and then glanced up and down the street, probably trying to decide where I had come from, or where I was going. "I am picking him up from a friend's house."

"Oh!" I said too loudly and with too much enthusiasm. "Do you guys live close by?' The last three words I spoke blended together creating one long sloppy word.

I knew I blew it.

Kevin started to answer my question pointing down the street when Payton abruptly stopped him. "We live close enough," she answered slowly, eyeing me suspiciously. "Are you drunk?" she asked.

"No!" I said defensively.

"You're not?" Payton asked sarcastically. "I can't believe I was actually trying to help you."

"What?" I said quietly.

"I felt bad for treating you badly, and I was trying to be that "friend" to help push you toward changing."

Silence and the occasional cricket was all I heard. It was that incredibly uncomfortable and awkward silence that seems to last too long. I could tell that Payton had a lot on her mind and am ashamed to admit that I was relieved she kept it to herself. I wouldn't have been able to handle anymore.

Payton looked over at her brother and attempted to smile, "Let's get you home." She couldn't hide the sadness in her voice.

"Payton ... I don't know what to tell you," I began, sounding weak and pathetic.

"I just thought there was more to you. I invested time in thinking that all you needed was a little encouragement and some real facts." She shook her head. "I guess I was wrong."

"This is who I am," I shouted. "If you don't like it, you should stop wasting so much of your precious time."

Payton's eyes widened at my aggressiveness. "I won't be wasting another second," she shot back.

I didn't want her to give up on me, not just yet, but my pride claimed every last inch of me. "Good," I said coldly, "Now I'll be able to focus my attentions on people who like me, just the way I am."

I had had so much turmoil building inside of me, that this was my release and Payton was the innocent victim, a casualty caught in the line of fire. I don't remember if I continued to yell at her or if I stood in silence as everything I had wanted to say screamed around in my head.

Somewhere in the middle of my tantrum, her face fell; she wasn't angry anymore. Payton looked at her brother for a long time, who looked confused to see his sister so emotional, then looked at me and whispered, "Did you even think of me at all before you did it?"

ꝏ

I walked the three blocks home as slowly as I could. My alcohol induced haze was nearly gone and the full reality of what had happened that night hit me like a ton of bricks. I hadn't planned on making two girls cry in one night.

I felt guilty.

I tried to enjoy the spring night air, but found it difficult. I remember thinking that my moral compass had to be broken. I was without direction, wandering lost, and now the only person who was trying to find me had just given up. I thought hard about Payton and what she had asked me before she left. The question I didn't answer.

Did I think about her at all?

I thought about her all the time. She consumed most of my thoughts, even random ones. She seemed to always be on my mind, but she wasn't that night. Actually, she was the furthest thing from my mind while I sat on that sofa at Derek's house. I don't know if that would give her any solace in knowing. And I don't know if she would even believe me if I told her that thinking about the people who would be disappointed in me was not an option. Thinking of her, Lynn, or my mom, would have killed me. I was only thinking of those people who were accepting of my actions.

I made it home without even realizing it. I sat on the steps in front of my house, trying to collect my thoughts. My curfew wasn't for another hour, but all I wanted was to crawl into my bed and sleep all of Sunday away. I became even more exhausted when I thought of having to wake up early that next morning so I could get my car back without anybody noticing.

"Tonight really sucked," I mumbled to myself as I quietly tiptoed through my dark house to my bedroom.

I flipped on my bedroom light and before my eyes could focus I heard my dad say, “We need to talk!”

Nine

He and my mom had been waiting for me. The mattress to my bed was off and flipped against the wall. My dad was sitting on the box spring, next to my no longer hidden stash. He was wearing sweatpants and looked like he had been sleeping. My mom sat in the back corner of my room at my desk. She was holding two creased papers in her hand. One was white the other pink.

My stomach plummeted.

My dad slowly picked up each one of the bottles, silently examining them. "You were out late throwing balls with your teammates," he said gruffly. "Did you get a lot of practicing in?"

I knew he was calling my bluff. His eyes pierced through me. "A little," I answered.

"A little?" he asked, "well, then how did you spend the rest of your night?" His voice was shaky, and I knew he wanted nothing more than to ring my neck.

I was defeated, and so very tired. I was tired of hiding. "At a party," I paused, and then added, "drinking."

My dad's face was hard to read. He stared at the bottles on my bed for a long time. I could hear my mom quietly sniffling, but I chose not to look at her. "I see," my dad said. He sounded more in control of his emotions. "I acknowledge your honesty; however, your actions deserve consequences."

"Yes sir," I said. I was just confirming what everyone in the room already knew. It was then that I started to realize that lying wasn't always the best alternative.

"I'm not going to lecture you on the stupidity of what you are doing, because I think you may actually realize this," my dad said as he pulled a black garbage bag from his pocket and started putting the bottles into it and added, "Don't expect to be leaving the house much these next few weeks; we will decide when you can leave and how long you will be gone for. You have also lost any privacy you may have thought you had. And I will personally be checking every inch of your room whenever I feel like it." My dad tied a knot at the top of the bag, the bottles clanked loudly together. It was an embarrassing sound.

I finally got the courage to look at my mom. She was reading the papers in her hands, probably for the hundredth time.

"Now, you are our only son," my dad began. My face flushed, I hated it when he brought that up. It felt weird to hear, and it had to feel weird for him to say. My mom cringed. "And we expected more from you, and you have disappointed us."

It looked like the lecturing was going to happen regardless.

"If we ever find something in your room again, or hear that you have done something stupid at one of those pointless parties again, so help me, you will regret it." My dad's temper was rising.

I continued to stand quietly in my doorway. I was beaten down and didn't have any fight left in me. I didn't even have the strength to bring up my father's own poor example locked away in his office's filing cabinet. I just took it, because even though my dad may have been a hypocrite at the time, my mom didn't deserve it. And I knew I was wrong. My silent demeanor ended the lecture. He looked like he had accomplished what he had set out to do. We all sat not looking at each other for what felt like an eternity.

"Who wrote these?" my mom finally asked, shattering the silence. I felt physically ill that my parents had found the alcohol but was incredibly embarrassed that they had found and read the notes from Payton. I wished I had thrown them away as soon as I had gotten them. And I hated that my face felt hot.

My dad quickly stepped in, "Kate, those don't matter. We're done here, let's go to bed." He stood and walked past me and out the door, carrying the garbage bag with him.

"Okay," my mom said, even though my dad had already left the room. She walked up to me and gently placed the papers into my hands. "Don't throw these away," she said reading my thoughts. "Whoever wrote them seems to care a lot about you."

"Or is someone who sees all my faults," I added.

"No," my mom said with a smile, "this person sees exactly what your mother sees ... everything you really are, inside." She started to cry.

"How did you find it?" I asked sadly, looking over at my upturned mattress.

"Oh," my mom's head dropped, "well, before B.J. left he mentioned baseball and how he loves the sport, so Lynn and I wanted to show him your plaques and trophies."

"So everyone knows?"

"No, I mean I don't think so," she said. "I ran into your room before they could get there to try and clean up a bit, I was gathering up dirty laundry under your bed and noticed the pink piece of paper sticking out from your mattress." I could tell she felt guilty for snooping around. "I also found the other things. I waited until later to show your father. At first I wasn't going to tell him what I had found, I just didn't know what to do." She cried harder.

I gave her a weak hug. "I'm so sorry, Mom." I felt unqualified to comfort her, since I was the cause of her pain. I thought about Payton, and then added, "I just want you to know that I didn't do this to hurt you. What I'm trying to say is, I didn't choose to do what I have been doing just because you didn't want me to, if that makes any sense," I said while shaking my head. It was difficult finding the right words to express what I was trying to say.

My mom nodded. "I know that you have a lot of pressure on you Jared, I also know that you are better than the person you've become," she said before kissing me on the forehead.

"I don't."

My mom looked at me with such conviction that I couldn't hold her gaze for long. "Someone once said that reputation is what others think you are, personality is what you seem to be, and character is what you really are," she said before leaving me alone in my room.

I flipped my mattress back on my bed and flopped face first on it. I hadn't changed clothes. I even had my shoes still on, but was planning on calling it a night and not moving a muscle until tomorrow morning, when I heard my bathroom door creak open.

"What do you need?" I said. My voice was muffled from the comforter.

"Is it true?"

"Is what true?" I asked, trying to sound naive.

"I heard everything, Jared!" Lynn shouted. I didn't move. She walked over to the bed and kicked my leg. I still didn't move. Lynn let out a frustrated scream, and then yelled, "I hate you! You ruined my entire night with B.J."

I flipped off my bed, held out my hands defensively. "I'm so sorry I ruined your date with that loser," I yelled.

"You of all people are calling *him* a loser?" she said, laughing out loud. "I guess it takes one to know one."

"Cute!" I sneered as I threw off my tennis shoes, "This attitude of yours is very becoming."

"Now, B.J. probably thinks our family is a bunch of freaks. Luckily he didn't see anything, but mom was acting so weird. After that, B.J. left, saying that he was going to give us some 'family time'. I'm just so embarrassed."

I was getting tired of hearing Lynn's problems and had already grown tired of hearing B.J.'s name. Even with her angry at me, I still didn't have the heart to tell her that tonight never was a date, at least in her guest's eyes.

"You guys should have never come in my room in the first place," I said instead, which got more of a reaction than I thought it would.

"Why? So you could continue drinking and partying? Because that seems to have been going so well for you," she said holding up the notes from Payton that I had set on my nightstand.

"Leave those alone!" I ran around the bed to grab them out of her hand. She willingly gave them to me then flopped down on my floor and buried her head in her hands and sobbed.

I listened to Lynn cry while looking at the papers crumpled in my fist, for a long time. My chest hurt deep inside.

"I was so scared," Lynn choked and then looked up at me. Her blond hair was stuck to the sides of her face.

I couldn't find my voice.

"When I heard Mom and Dad talking as they waited for you, I was so mad, but I was more scared. I knew where you were going tonight, because I overheard you talking to your friends." Lynn rubbed her nose on her pajama sleeve. "I swore you were dead somewhere and I would never see you again," she cried.

I went and sat down next to my sister. I gently put my arms around her and said, "I don't want you to have to ever worry about something like that." She rested her head on my shoulder. "I'm sorry," I said.

We sat there for a long time. I thought about a lot of things until I could hear Lynn deeply breathing next to me. I picked her up and carried her back to her room. I laid her on her bed and then whispered into her ear, "Please, promise me you won't ever be dumb like me."

"I promise," Lynn said sleepily as I went to leave her room. She smiled without ever opening her eyes and then pulled her white comforter up to her neck.

Ten

"Now that we have finished talking about preparation," Mrs. Flint said cheerfully, "we will move on to the more pleasant, action stage, and our long anticipated group project!"

My stomach knotted.

I felt in the minority because people seemed excited for this project. I wondered if I were the only one in the class who was terrified to hear about the time and energy people have to sacrifice when they are actively changing their behavior and environment.

"Those who enter both the preparation and action stages need to be fully committed to the cause. They have reached their limit and know that something needs to change and they are ready to make that change no matter what," said Mrs. Flint.

I half-heartedly jotted down what she was saying, as I thought about Lynn sobbing on my floor and my mom's broken heart, both caused by me. I also thought about Payton.

I could hear Payton's pencil swiftly scratching her paper. The tension was there between us as usual, and I hated it. The back of my head felt hot and I imagined that it was from her laser-like glare. Or maybe I just hoped it was. Any look would have been better than the last one I saw from her pretty face, the look before she drove away leaving me alone in the street.

I had wanted to talk to her so badly when I had walked into class. I hated how things had gotten progressively worse between the two of us. It only took me a few seconds to realize how closed off she was. I probably was the last person she wanted to sit behind and talking to me seemed undoubtedly out of the question, but how could she feel any differently toward me. I did know that her body language was screaming, "Stay away!"

On the other hand, Kim had been trying to act uninterested and occupied during Mrs. Flint's lecture, but was doing a horrible job of it. She intentionally turned her body so that she could see me better without trying to be obvious.

"Now's the time to put into 'action'," Mrs. Flint said with air parentheses, "what we have been learning." She laughed to herself. "For the last fifteen minutes of class, I would like each of you to pick something in your life that you would like to change and write it down. Then I want you to list things you could be doing in your life to help you make that change." Mrs. Flint started handing out large manila folders. "On each of these folders is a number. That is now your assigned number for this project, so don't forget it."

Mine was fourteen. I grabbed the folder off my desk and looked inside. There was a lined piece of paper with some writing on it. "I have paired each one of you with a student from one of my afternoon classes. Every correspondence you will have with each other will be anonymous unless you decide otherwise," she continued.

I for sure wasn't going to reveal my true identity regardless of what I decided to write about.

"What are we supposed to do with the paper that is already in the folder," Payton asked. I sighed. The sound of her voice captivated me. I just wished she would talk to me.

Derek pulled out the paper inside his folder and read aloud in a high pitched whiny voice, "I want to change the way I treat my best friend." Derek laughed loudly, "What is this junk?"

The girl sitting in front of Derek shook her head and mumbled something about him being an inconsiderate jerk. Derek leaned closer to the back of her head and whispered, "Oh, I'm sorry did they copy your idea?"

"Mr. Dixon," Mrs. Flint said sternly, "These are not to be shared with the class, they must be kept confidential. If you can't do that, then I guess you will have to receive a zero for the project."

"Nope, that won't be necessary. I will protect it with my life," Derek said dramatically as he slid the paper back into the folder and slowly sealed it then tucked it protectively under his arm.

Mrs. Flint peered at Derek a second more and then said, "I would like everyone to take this seriously. I would like you to discreetly read what your partner has written," she pointed a finger at Derek, "and then comment. Give some positive feedback, give advice, or suggestions on how to help them make their change. And they will do the same for you."

I slowly pulled the piece of paper out of the folder. I had gotten too curious, and noticed that most of the class was doing the same. "I want to change someone's life," was written on the top. I gawked at the paper. I felt angry that I had been paired with someone who felt they didn't need to change anything about themselves but wanted to fix things that were wrong with other people.

"Your grade for this assignment will be based on an evaluation filled out by your partner. They will decide if you have been sincere in this assignment and have made strides in changing yourself. And your partner's grade will be determined by each of your evaluations," Mrs. Flint said excitedly.

I didn't have high hopes for my partners' grade, and was a little worried about mine. *What was I going to try to change? Or better yet, what was I willing to admit I needed to change?* Class was almost over and I needed to come up with something quick. Mrs. Flint was starting to collect our folders. It was depressing to realize that there were so many things I needed to improve on. I wondered what Payton was writing about, and how hard it probably was for her to come up with a single thing.

"I want to change the way I pick up girls," Derek whispered to me.

I avoided turning completely around and said over my shoulder, "Good one! I'm pretty sure *that* will earn you a passing grade."

"I'm serious," Derek laughed, "And I don't appreciate your sarcasm." I thought he was done but after a few long seconds he added, "Or maybe I'll change the way the world plays beer pong!"

I shook my head. "Well, which brilliant idea are you going to go with?"

"Both!" Derek said quickly, "They're both so great ... I can't choose."

I turned my focus to my own paper. I thought about next year when I would be a senior, and wondered if things were going to be the same, if *I* were going to be the same. My mom knew I was a better person than I had become.

Did I?

I hunched over my paper and quickly wrote "I want to change my future," and then quickly stuffed it into the envelope with the other paper and handed it to Mrs. Flint as she walked by. Class ended and as I was grabbing my back pack off of the back of my chair, Kim looked at me and said, "You look good today."

"Thanks," I said. I knew that she wasn't expecting me to tell her right this second what my decision was, if I had decided to give us a try or not, but it felt like she wanted something more from me than just a "thanks." Kim even looked different today. She was wearing more clothes and less make up, almost like she were trying to emulate someone. I was such a jerk, and didn't deserve either her or Payton.

Kim stood in front of me and people had to walk around us to get out the door. Payton was one of those people. "Um, well, I will see you later then," Kim said awkwardly.

"Okay," I said, watching Payton walk down the hall. She never once looked back at me.

The rest of the day went by in slow motion. Knowing that I would finally be able to go to baseball practice was the only thing getting me through the day. During lunch, Kim went to sit with some of her other friends. When questioned, Derek said that she was probably trying to give me more space. So it was just Derek, me and a few of the guys from the team.

I didn't talk much.

"I heard that your party was pretty sick, bro!" Gus said, as soon as he sat down at the table. "I heard some guys talking about you and two girls, and how they wished they could have gotten half as much action as you did."

Derek just sat back in his chair smirking and then said, "No one can ever get as lucky as I did."

"It's true?" Gus asked, his eyes wide with surprise, and then quickly shook his head. "No! I don't believe it."

"Sure is, just go ask Brandi and Amanda." Derek smiled.

Gus looked at me for some kind of confirmation. Raising my eyebrows, I nodded slightly, and then shrugged trying to indicate that though it was indeed true, I too, found it hard to believe.

"What? I can't believe I missed it!" Gus yelled. "I miss everything!"

"Make sure you don't miss the lake party this Saturday then, both girls are supposed to be there." Derek pointed at me and said, "Don't think we have forgotten about your birthday, bro,"

So he hadn't forgotten. I felt flustered and was aware of Derek and the rest of the guys watching me.

"I really don't care to do anything for my birthday," I paused trying to look convincing. "I would skip the day entirely if I could." I was the only one who knew about the new restrictions my parents had placed on me, and I preferred to keep it that way. I didn't want them thinking I was anything but serious about doing absolutely nothing that weekend, when deep down I knew that there was no way I would be leaving my house without a fight.

"What!" exclaimed Gus.

"I'm with you, man," Derek said to Gus, "For my birthday, we will be celebrating all week long."

"And I will be there."

"My mom is trying to plan some family thing, I think. I just want to relax and do nothing," I interrupted. I still wasn't sure if my mom had planned anything, but was counting on the possibility.

"Not if I have anything to say about it." Derek grinned. "I'm going to call your mom and tell her I have a little get-together planned for Saturday at one. So you better meet me at the marina."

I started to panic. "I'll talk to her," I said quickly. I needed some time to figure out what to do. "Just don't get your hopes up," I added.

"It will only be a few people, just the team and a few select females," Derek said and then laughed when Gus and a few other guys started cheering loudly.

I shook my head, almost hoping my dad would stay home for the weekend. It would at least keep me from getting in anymore trouble, because I knew it would be easier to sneak out and go to the party on my mom's watch. The idea of people getting together to celebrate my birth was enticing but I think a part of me really wanted to just stay home and accept my punishment peacefully. I hated feeling obligated. After all, it was a party for me. I just felt too exhausted to pretend to be somebody I wasn't so sure was worth being anymore.

"I've talked to Kim about it, she's in, if it's okay with you?" Derek said. "She has some pretty good ideas. She has even made flyers to give to the people we want to invite, I mean ... you want to invite." This had already gone too far. Apparently everyone else was on the same page regarding my birthday, except me.

Derek read my expression and quickly jumped in, "This really wasn't my idea at all. Kim has kind of taken charge and is really trying. She has put a lot of work into this. Just humor her, will you? Please!"

I knew that Derek needed this weekend as much as Kim did. He was thinking about two blonde cheerleaders and Kim was thinking about me. And I, well, I was thinking about nobody, not even myself, which was why I didn't say no. I didn't answer either way, which was enough of an answer for Derek.

Hardly able to hold in his excitement, Derek followed me to my next class, "Who should Kim invite?" he asked.

"I couldn't care less," I said slowly.

"We'll keep it small," Derek shouted as he walked away, "You won't regret it!"

Mr. Atwood, was passing me in the hall and paused, he looked at Derek leaving and then back at me. "What won't you regret?" he asked suspiciously.

"Something I'm already regretting," I said. I turned and walked into my class not waiting to see his reaction.

ꙮ

I was early to practice. The other guys were messing around in the locker room, still changing. I had gotten tired of listening to Derek talk about what he and Kim were planning for the lake party, so I told Derek that I was going to go warm up in the bull pen.

Instead I stood on the pitcher's mound. I held a baseball in my glove and slowly rotated my right arm back and forth. It felt so much better and it was a relief knowing that I would be throwing again. I needed to have something else to concentrate on, something that made me feel happy no matter how bad a day I had. Baseball was that thing.

"You want to throw the ball around before practice starts?"

I had been so lost in my thoughts that I didn't notice I was no longer the only one on the field. "Sure," I said quickly turning toward the dug-out.

B.J. was standing with a glove on his hand, wearing white baseball pants and a grey New York Yankees tee shirt. It was identical to the one I had on. They had been my favorite team since I was a little boy. His shirt even had a bleach stain on the sleeve, just like the one I had back home on my floor somewhere.

"Err, your mom lent me some of your baseball clothes the other day," B.J. said, grabbing the front of his shirt. "I hope you don't mind."

"Don't mind?" I seethed.

"So, what about catch?" he asked, ignoring my anger.

Speaking of catching, this kid always seemed to catch me off guard and had a knack for getting under my skin and staying there. I stormed toward him. I wanted him to take a few steps back; that would at least prove he was intimidated, but he didn't. He actually took a few steps closer, quickly closing the gap between us.

He met my gaze without blinking.

Derek and the rest of the team were making their way through the gate to the infield. I watched them walk closer to us. B.J. never took his eyes off of me. "Hey! It looks like you met B.J.," Derek said to me, slapping B.J. playfully on the back. "How are you, my man?"

"I'm doing great! Ready to play," B.J. answered Derek, while still staring at me.

"I hope you are ready for this guy's curve ball," Derek told him, as he pointed to me.

"I've been looking forward to it." B.J. smiled at me, and then finally broke his stare. "I'm going to go stretch." He ran to the grass near right field where the rest of the team was stretching.

"That guy's awesome," Derek said to me.

"How do you know him?" I yelled.

Derek looked confused by my outburst. He stared at me wide-eyed then said, "Last week. He started coming to practices toward the end of last week." Derek started shaking his finger, "That's right! You weren't here. He started coming the day after you hurt your shoulder. Coach really likes him; he has a killer swing, can hit almost anything! I think Coach is going to put him on Varsity."

I was so mad. "How could Coach do that? We have our team!" I snapped.

"He already talked to Justin about moving him down to designated hitter," Derek said. "Why are you so upset? We could use him. The season hasn't even started yet. You know as well as anyone that the teams aren't set in stone, at least not until next week when we play our first real game."

Derek was looking at me like I were insane. I felt insane. I was most likely going to be this year's team captain, and especially in that position I should want whatever is best for the team, and it seemed like everyone thought B.J. was just that. Unfortunately, I would have taken any member of my school's chess team to play with over B.J. I felt, on top of all the other crap going on, like he was slowly creeping into my life, imposing himself into every aspect of it.

"Let's get started boys," Coach Kline called to Derek and me. He was leaning against the chain link fence near where everyone was stretching. He was talking to Leo, our assistant coach, who had a large clip board in his hand. "Today is going to double as a regular practice and tryouts in a way," he told us after we had finished stretching. "There are a few new boys who have come out this year, and they deserve a chance to earn their spots on this team."

At that Coach Kline told us to break into pairs and play catch for a while to warm up our arms. I went to go stand by Derek when Coach yelled, "Jared! You and your twin pair up."

I looked down at my shirt and groaned.

B.J. ran over, so he was standing across from me and gave me a satisfied smile. I threw the ball at him harder than I would have normally. He caught it with ease, and fired the ball back, just as hard. I clenched my teeth. I wasn't about to let up now. I wouldn't be the first to back down. I sent a rocket to B.J, and was happy to see his face wince when the ball hit his glove.

"I was thinking," I said loudly, "I will probably start tutoring Lynn in math now, so you can find someone else to take on as a project, or whatever it is you are doing with my sister." I was feeling confident now.

He threw the ball back and it lightly smacked my glove. I think he realized that I could out throw him and ended the competition. "I think we should let Lynn decide that." B.J. smiled widely. "I'm pretty sure she won't want help from someone who isn't that good at math."

He was right, I sucked at math. I growled and then threw the ball so hard that it flung out of my hand early. It flew over B.J.'s head smacking the chain link fence behind him, just as Coach Kline and Leo were walking by. Coach Kline ducked in just enough time. "Watch it!" he yelled.

B.J. ran over to the fence, scooped up the ball and said, "Sorry about that Coach, it was my fault."

"Keep an eye on it, boy. Jared's got an arm on him."

"I'll try," B.J. said and then patted Coach on the arm. "Good thing you have quick reflexes." B.J. and Coach Kline both laughed.

I walked away, ending my warm up early. I had had enough of this guy.

Coach had us run a few different drills, and then hit some ground balls to us to see how our fielding was doing. B.J. did better than I had wanted him to. He said he felt most comfortable on second base, and it showed. The last half hour of practice Coach wanted to watch the team bat, so he decided to let me pitch to them, and told me to hold nothing back. This was what I had been waiting for.

"How do you like that?" I taunted Derek after I struck him out. He pretended to rush the mound. I waved to him as he walked to the bench.

I was starting to feel better. I struck out three other guys after Derek, and Gus popped one up in the infield, then B.J. came up to bat. I wanted to strike him out so badly I could taste it. Both Coach Kline and Leo were watching intently and whispering, but it was B.J. they were focused on, not me.

"I'll give you a show. We'll see how well your new hopeful does when he tries to hit my curve ball," I mumbled to myself. And that's what I threw. B.J. completely fell for it, his bat cut through the empty air as my ball dropped suddenly to the ground.

"Nice swing!" yelled Leo. "If you connect, that ball's out of here."

I was worried about that same thing. B.J. did have a strong, solid swing. I just needed to be smarter and faster. My next pitch was a fast ball. The ball's speed increased drastically from my previous pitch. B.J. read it wrong and swung too late, another strike.

I was getting cocky. I wanted to strike him out on what I was "famous" for, another curve ball. The thought of watching him swing as my ball suddenly curved inside and toward him hard made me almost giddy. I placed my pointer and middle fingers on the left side of the seam, and flicked my wrist hard just as I released the baseball.

It reached him in less than a second, but I could see B.J. watching the ball intently, never taking his eyes off of it. Instead of swinging when I hoped he would, as the ball was coming straight for his bat, he waited. And instead of waiting for the ball to hit the catcher's glove and getting another pitch, he tucked his elbows closer to his body and swung just as the ball jerked toward him.

I watched the second person to hit a homerun on me this year, run to me to shake my hand. I refused. "Good job! You almost had me on the last pitch," B.J. said innocently. He started walking to the dug-out where Derek and the rest of the team were chanting his name, then turned and added, "Jared, you are very talented."

I wanted to say something insulting back, but everybody was watching.

"Thanks," I said grudgingly. Unfortunately he did just prove why he deserved to be on the team, as much as I hated to see it happen.

I wasn't in the mood to stick around after practice. Coach Kline announced who had made the varsity team and I wasn't surprised to hear B.J.'s name called. The team then voted on a captain, I also wasn't surprised to hear that I had been chosen. I just hoped that I could still lead the team while hating one of its players.

I threw my bat bag into the back seat and started my car. I had three missed calls from Lynn and five from my mom. It wasn't like either one of them to call me when I was at practice, especially that many times. I scrolled through the call history option on my phone one more time and noticed that I had a voicemail from my dad.

My heart stopped, something was wrong. He never called me.

"Jared," my dad's recorded voice rang hollowly into my ear, "we are at the hospital, fourth floor... room thirteen."

I dropped my cell phone onto the passenger seat, threw my car into reverse. I could still hear old voicemail messages quietly playing as I recklessly punched the gas pedal, quickly backing out of my parking space. In my rearview mirror I saw B.J. jump out of the way of my car and then chase after me, waving his hands above his head as my car screeched out of the parking lot. I never slowed down once as I headed toward Boulder City Hospital.

Eleven

The dimly lit hospital room felt ironically inviting. Machines quietly beeped and hummed, slowly putting me to sleep. My Grandpa was lying in the hospital bed, the large gown he wore made his shoulders and arms look so frail and tiny. He had tubes coming out of his nose. The nurse said it was helping him breathe. My mom had said that throughout the day my grandpa's fever had progressively gotten worse. Shortly after getting him comfortable in his recliner in front of the television, she had decided to check on him and that was when she found him, slumped over and unconscious.

It had probably been an entire hour since anyone had said anything to each other. Grandpa was still unconscious and in a possible coma, at least that is what the doctors thought. Lynn was asleep on the tiny sofa in the room. Her head was in my mom's lap and my mom slowly ran her hands through Lynn's hair. My dad couldn't sit still for long and had been in and out of the room a dozen times. He had made a comment about going down to the cafeteria to get a bite to eat. We hadn't seen him for almost two hours.

"Excuse me," Dr. Gardner said as he popped his head in the door. My mom waved him in. Dr. Gardner, in a way, was a part of our family. He had been our physician since before I was born. We respected him. I respected him.

Dr. Gardner looked at me and smiled, "How are you buddy?" he asked.

I just nodded.

My mom left my grandpa's side to give Dr. Gardner a hug. "What's the verdict, Bruce?" she asked. Her voice sounded strained and exhausted.

I could tell he was reluctant talking about any kind of results with my mother while I was in the room listening. My mom looked at me and then over at Lynn who was snoring quietly, and then back at Dr. Gardner, "It's okay, go ahead," she said calmly. She walked over to where I was sitting and slowly rubbed my back.

"All right," Dr. Gardner said and then cleared his throat. "Your father's blood results are a cause of concern for me, and some of the ultrasound tests are indicating possible cancerous growths in a number of locations." Dr. Gardner paused to see if we were following him.

My mom let out a muffled moan. "So it's back," she quickly said.

"It looks like it, and it's spreading quickly."

"How long ...?" My mom couldn't finish her sentence.

"Maybe two months, if he's lucky," Dr. Gardner said sadly. He sat quietly, waiting for this news to sink in, waiting to see if we had any questions. "You know I hate being the bearer of bad news."

He had delivered devastating news to our family before. News that was probably a lot harder to handle. Being an eighty five year old man, Grandpa Miller had lived a full life. It would be hard to let him go, but it was the natural order of things. There is nothing natural about having to bury your baby. If my parents could handle that, we should be able to handle this. Unfortunately I worried that my parents hadn't really coped with my brother's death and were a gentle push away from going over the edge. Actually, *I* felt like that most the time and I barely remembered Bryce.

So what hope did we have then?

"Hello, Michael. How are you holding up?" Dr. Gardner asked as my dad came back into the room a few minutes later.

"Fine," he said, holding the door open wide, "we have a visitor." My dad's expression was hard to read.

B.J. walked into the room. He was still wearing his baseball pants and my matching shirt. I knew I should have changed before coming here, I was just so stressed that I sped to the hospital as fast as I could.

"Who's this?" Dr. Gardner asked. "He looks like he belongs with your family. Actually, you two look like you could be twins,"

He said pointing to both B.J. and me. Dr. Gardner shook B.J.'s hand as he introduced himself.

"Apparently my clothes are now community property," I said. "I looked ridiculous in front of my team."

My mom mouthed the words "sorry" to me, and then explained that B.J. was a friend of Lynn's from school.

"Jared didn't tell me you were on the baseball team," my dad said to B.J., who looked shocked to hear my dad speak to him. I think we were all a little stunned.

"That's because he wasn't, at least not until today," I said, before B.J. could find his voice.

"Coach Kline just told me that I would be on the varsity team today," B.J. explained.

"Hmm," was all my dad said, but it seemed enough for B.J. He was grinning from ear to ear. I, of course was irritated, once again.

"I don't want to keep you from visiting and having some family time," Dr. Gardner said, before excusing himself. "I'll let you know the other test results as soon as they come in."

As soon as he left the room, my mom told my dad that the results were in and that she wanted to discuss them with him in private. My dad asked a few general questions, questions that didn't require her to go into a lot of detail. B.J. sat at the chair closest to the giant monitor with different lines and numbers on it. He looked up at the metal stand next to the bed and gently touched the plastic IV bag full of what looked like water.

"B.J., don't worry about that sweetie, it's just liquid to keep my dad hydrated," my mom said, interrupting her conversation with my dad.

"Oh, okay," he said.

My mom picked right back up from where she had left off and I grabbed my headphones from my pocket. I needed to get away from reality for a second. It was funny how music could sometimes transport me to another place, away from some of my worries, at least for a while.

I'm not sure how long I had been listening, it could have been only a few minutes but I had day dreamed about being drafted into the major leagues, by the Yankees, none the less. I was still grinning to myself when B.J. suddenly stood and walked over to the hospital bed. He sat on the edge and peered down at my grandpa. It felt weird watching this interaction. It was too intimate for a random acquaintance, if that, to be so close to my unconscious grandpa. I didn't even feel it was appropriate having him in the room at all, but seemed to be the only one who felt that way.

B.J. looked like he was talking. I pulled the headphones out of my ears and looked around. Lynn was still asleep on the sofa, but my mom and dad were no longer in the room. I hadn't noticed them leave.

"You still have more to do. It's not time, yet." I heard B.J. whisper. "She is excited to see you again, but knows that there is still more you have to do. She misses you but wants you to hold on a little longer."

"What are you doing?" I snapped.

B.J. jumped, startled by my outburst.

I didn't give him any time before yelling again. "I asked you a question! What were you doing?" I found it hard to control myself. He had been whispering so quietly that is was hard to make out exactly everything he had been saying but I got the gist of it and didn't like it.

Lynn moaned and sat up on the sofa, "Why are you yelling," she whined. Her eyes were still half closed. She stretched and then noticed B.J. She yelped and then grabbed at her hair trying to smooth it down which was nearly impossible after my mom had been playing with it.

"I didn't know you were here." Lynn giggled.

"Zip it, Lynn," I snapped. She stuck her tongue out at me. I ignored her, jumped up from the chair and walked over to the hospital bed. I pointed my finger at B.J., and was getting ready to let him have it. Everything I was feeling inside about him, and had been for a while, was threatening to explode from me; that was until I saw my grandpa, his eyes were open revealing that brown color with specks of yellow, I had grown to love.

"Oh," I whispered quietly as I stared down at him, but he never took his eyes off of B.J. "Gramps', can you hear me?" I asked as I grabbed his hand and squeezed it gently.

Lynn was now standing at the foot of the hospital bed, her face probably mirrored mine; she looked excited and relieved. "How long has he been awake?" she asked B.J.

"Just a few minutes," B.J. whispered soothingly, never breaking eye contact with my grandpa. "He's going to probably slip back into a deep sleep again." B.J. said it so matter-of-factly that I wasn't sure how to react. "You should probably go get your parents," he said to me, pointing to the door, "They're just in the hallway." I didn't like taking orders from this kid, but knew that he was right, my parents needed to know.

"When?" I heard my Grandpa mumble as I scrambled to open the door.

"Soon, just not now," B.J said right before I yelled at my mom and dad, who were standing a few feet from the door.

Horror shone on my mom's face as she pushed past me, "Dad," she sobbed as she ran to his bed.

"He's fine," my dad said rubbing my mom's back, as she scanned the monitors feverishly, watching his vital signs.

"What? He is?" My mom sighed deeply. "I thought something was wrong." She grabbed her chest and took several deep breaths.

"Mrs. Anderson," B.J. said as he pointed to my grandpa, "he's awake."

My mom looked down just as his eyes were closing, "Not now, but soon," he mumbled again before slipping back into unconsciousness.

"Dad, can you hear me? It's Kate ... your daughter," my mom asked enthusiastically.

He didn't answer and didn't wake back up. My mom and dad went to inform the nurses and Doctor Gardner about what had just happened, and left with strict instructions that if Grandpa were to wake up again we needed to call my mom immediately.

"Who do you think you are?" I asked B.J. as soon as my parents left. I felt a pain deep within me. I couldn't understand why my grandpa would choose to talk to B.J. and not me. Why did this stranger get that chance, over me, Lynn, and better yet, my mom?

"What are you talking about, Jared?" Lynn asked. She had moved, so now she was standing within a few inches of B.J.

"You are way too involved with my family, and I want to know why!" I said. I sat down on the sofa Lynn had been sleeping on, spread my arms across the back cushions and stared B.J. down, letting him know that I wasn't planning on going anywhere until I got some answers.

"I don't know what you want to hear? Lynn left me a message about your Grandpa and I thought I would come and ..."

"That's the problem!" I interrupted. "You genuinely think it is all right for you to be here!"

"Jared!" Lynn said, "You're being rude."

"No, he's right," B.J said to Lynn. "I'll see you at school tomorrow."

"That's another thing." I wasn't finished yet. "I think it would be in your best interest if you found someone else to spend time with, besides Lynn."

"Stop it now, Jared!" Lynn screamed. "It's none of your business."

"I'm just trying to protect you, Lynn."

"From what?" she cried.

"Do you really think this guy wants to date you? I think he is just using you," I said. "And he better believe it won't happen anymore!" I pointed my finger at B.J.

Lynn looked devastated. She refused to look at either one of us. B.J. on the other hand looked totally caught off guard. "I don't ... I mean, I uh, those aren't my intentions at all," he stammered. "She's a sister to me," he said reverently, and then looked down at Lynn intently.

She had clammed up, her head was down and her arms were protectively tucked to her chest. She looked like she was caving in on herself. B.J's reaction was clear to me that his objectives, at least regarding my sister, were innocent. And now, they were also clear to Lynn. I could see the realization of Lynn's true feelings toward B.J. hit him right upside the head. Lynn's hopeful plans she had been entertaining were now exposed.

I couldn't take back what I had said. I was surprised that I wished to. I just didn't like seeing what I had done to Lynn. "I'm sorry," I said meekly, "I know it sounds like a weak apology, but I mean it."

"You completely humiliated me," she said, still not looking up.

"Do you want to go for a walk, so we can talk," B.J asked quietly.

"No," Lynn answered quickly, "I just want to be alone." She walked over to me, grabbed her purse from the sofa, and left the room.

"This is your fault!" I turned to B.J., as soon as the door shut. I didn't want to waste any time before getting in a few more jabs and I also needed to pass off some of the blame.

"I know," he said sadly. "I should have picked up on it. I was too focused on trying to take care of her and protect her, that I missed the signs." B.J. slowly walked to the door. I didn't have to say another word. He was doing my job for me, by beating himself up. "Now I've caused more harm than good." He looked at me, like he was expecting some advice or maybe some words of comfort.

He wasn't getting either from me. "Yes! You have," I said loudly. "I can be enough of a protection for her. Now will you leave us alone?"

B.J. nodded and left.

I had gotten rid of him, and without much effort. I was actually shocked at how easy it had been. I just needed to be a little ruthless. The last thing I needed to do was seal the deal. I didn't want him sneaking back into our family and causing more problems for me.

I found Lynn in the courtyard. She had obviously been crying. The tip of her nose was raw, probably from her rubbing it too much. The tears on her eyelashes made her eyes sparkle. I remember thinking, again, how pretty she was becoming. I reminded myself that I was doing this for her. I may have just found out that B.J. wasn't romantically interested in her, but I still had an incredibly unsettling feeling whenever I was around him. There were just too many red flags.

I didn't know much about him and his life, he always seemed to direct the conversation elsewhere whenever it was brought up. He had singlehandedly inserted himself into our family's lives within a week. And, he was weird! He didn't act like other fifteen year olds. Unfortunately, I was the only one in my family who saw these flags. So I was forced to make some flags of my own that they would pay attention to.

I am not proud of what I did next, I had said the words before I had even fully decided if I was going to go through with it, and by then it was too late. I was already in too deep. I knew she would be hurt, but I also believed that she deserved to hear the truth.

"Lynn," I began, "please hear me out?"

She had started to get up. Apparently she didn't want my company either.

"B.J. was at my locker the day before he ever met you," I quickly said before she could leave. She sat back down. I cleared my throat and then let everything that had been building inside of me pour out. "He was just standing there staring at me. He obviously wanted to talk to me but I didn't give him the chance. This so called friend of yours has crept into my life. He joined my baseball team, and worse he has been using my sister to get to me."

"But that day in the lunch room, he came to help me," she pleaded. She sounded like a trial lawyer defending the integrity of her client. "It was like he came out of nowhere, offering friendship when no one else would. He was my angel." She blushed slightly and then cried even harder.

"Lynn," I said soothingly, hoping to soften the blow of my next statement, "he knew you were my sister, just like he knows where to always find me. When I rejected his attempt to meet me, he went after you. Inviting him into our home was just icing on the cake for him." I had successfully presenting my closing argument and unfortunately for Lynn there was too much evidence against B.J.

"Why?" was all Lynn could say before burying her face in her hands. I was too affected by what I was doing to her to say anything else.

She stayed down in the courtyard the entire time my family was there. My mom had tried several times to get her to go back up to Grandpa's room with her, but she wouldn't. She never told my mom anything, to which I was grateful. I think she also worried that my mom, too, would be hurt by B.J.'s deception.

I stayed in the courtyard. I stayed as long as she did. Most the time I watched her from a distance, giving her the space she needed. I'm not even sure she knew I was there.

Twelve

"Do you want to look at the flyers ... to see if you like them?" asked Kim. She was holding a large stack of bright blue papers. I could see my name across the top in bold letters. When I didn't take them from her, she let her arm drop to her side, and looked over at Derek.

"Come on, Jared, be a good sport," he said. Derek threw more than half of the hamburger he was holding onto a lunch tray, and said, "This is disgusting!"

"I thought you said it was going to be a 'little get-together'," I said, irritated. "Something you were going to keep small."

"I know." He grinned. "Boating on the lake is only going to be a few close friends. Those ...," he said, pointing to the stack of papers, "are for the after party!"

I threw an apple core into the garbage can behind Gus. He held his arms up as it flew over his head and into the plastic can. "Field goal!" he yelled loudly.

"Bobby said we could have it at his house," Derek said excitedly. He wiped his hands on a napkin and then walked over to where I was standing. "We've already passed out a stack twice that size," he said.

"You've got to be kidding me!" I yelled. I was starting to lose it. Other things were on my mind. Things like my grandpa's condition and the situation with Lynn were starting to change my perspective. Things that Derek and Kim, or anyone else for that matter, wouldn't understand. Things I would have never even told them in the first place.

"You know you want to go," Derek said. "I know you."

Apparently he didn't.

"Have fun this weekend without me, because I'm not going to be there," I fumed.

"What are you talking about, man?" Derek took another step closer to me as I stood. "What is going on? When have you ever not wanted to party with us? We're doing this for you!"

"I'm just over it," I said, sitting back down.

Kim set the flyers on the table and slumped down into a chair. She was obviously upset. Derek grabbed the stack of papers from her before she could throw them away, and said aggressively, "So what is it?"

"Excuse me?" I said mockingly.

"I'm just curious what you are planning on changing ... you know for the psychology project." Derek pointed around the table. "Is it your friends? Are you planning on changing your friends?" I didn't like the route this was going. Everybody was staring at me, most of them looked confused, but Kim's eyes widened and she nodded slightly, like she finally understood my behavior. "Or maybe your personality ... is that it?" he continued.

I just shook my head, "You're reading way too much into this, man."

"Or maybe it's just as simple as wanting to change how you spend your weekends. If that's the case, we should start partying on Wednesdays. Would that work for you?" Derek asked. I was getting tired of his sarcasm and was quickly losing patience. "Because I would hate to think that you would choose the first two for *just* a dumb school project." Derek exchanged a long glance with Kim before looking back at me. They both suspected that my actions were more calculated than Derek was accusing me of. Kim's cheeks reddened.

I decided to put an end to it. I pulled Derek aside and stated angrily, "This has nothing to do with Payton. I'm lower than dirt to her. So you can go skip on over to Kim and tell her that."

"Will do," Derek said. "But that still doesn't explain this weekend."

I took a deep breath and then said a little too loudly, "I got caught. Are you happy now?" I knew that Kim and the rest of the guys could hear, but at that point I didn't care. It was better than them knowing I was questioning myself, their friendship, and frankly everything about my life.

"Was it after my party?"

"No," I lied, "On Sunday, when I went back to get my car at your house. My parents questioned me and I told them I had been drinking the night before." It sounded less embarrassing than the truth.

Derek didn't say anything for a while. "I'm sorry, I shouldn't have lost my cool like that," he finally said.

"It's all right."

"At least your parents care enough to do something when they hear you have been drinking. I could leave evidence directly in front of my parents' noses and they would turn a blind eye to it," Derek whispered. "Don't get me wrong, I'm not complaining. I'm just saying their concern should mean something."

"Well, however you take the gesture. I am on indefinite lockdown for an undisclosed period of time."

"And there's no way you can sneak out?"

"It all depends on if my dad leaves town or not."

Derek understood completely. "Well, if he does leave town, just come to Lake Mead. There won't be any booze there." Derek clasped his hands together and got down on one knee begging me to come.

I felt sick inside, and could feel myself sweating. I was feeling the pressure and after all the effort they had put into that weekend, I couldn't justify not trying. I was still too worried about what everyone thought of me. "I'll try to be there," I finally said, hoping to feel some kind of relief, but getting none.

"That's what I'm talking about," Derek cheered loudly. He pumped his fist in the air as he walked back to the table with the flyers. "Keep passing those out," he said to Kim, who never took her eyes off of me the entire time.

"Okay," she said enthusiastically.

"I will catch up with you guys later, I'm going to meet up with Amanda," Derek paused, "or is it Brandi?"

"You're messed up," Gus said laughing, as I sat back down in my seat.

"No really, I'm serious, I can't remember which one." Derek winked at me.

"Well, here's to hoping you figure it out before you get there," Gus said holding up his water bottle as Derek left the cafeteria.

I still had ten more minutes before lunch was over and my Algebra class would start. I had a test that day and knew I should have been going over my homework and notes, since I wasn't prepared at all. Instead I looked around the lunchroom. I couldn't see Lynn anywhere, again. I needed to keep a better eye on her. I entertained the idea that maybe she had moved on and found a new group of friends and was off having a good time somewhere.

"Jared's birthday party, this Saturday, at Bobby's house, you're invited!" I heard Kim say. She was giving a flyer to someone I had never seen before.

I rolled my eyes and mumbled, "What have I done?"

She heard me. "If you would just relax and let us celebrate our *good friend's* birthday, you may actually have a good time." There was a defensive tone to her voice.

"Why? Is that because you'll be there?"

Kim blinked a few times, and her jaw tightened.

"I didn't mean to sound so condescending. I just said the first thing that came to my mind, obviously without thinking," I said.

She turned, continuing to pass out those stupid bright blue papers, in fact a little more generously than she probably would have otherwise.

I thumbed through my algebra book and started to review the Quadratic Formula, when I heard Kim say in a mocking tone, "You wouldn't want one of these, it's not your type of crowd."

"I wasn't asking for one." The voice made me look up. Payton was standing in front of Kim. She looked beautiful.

"Then why would you come over here?" Kim fanned herself with the flyers and stuck a hand on her hip, "if not to check out what we're planning for Jared's birthday."

Payton held up a paper lunch sack she had been holding and dramatically flung it into the trash can next to Kim. Payton smirked and said, "You guys shouldn't think so highly of yourselves," and then walked away after giving me one last glance.

"What a self-righteous witch," I heard Kim mumble.

I sat quietly for a while, just thinking, and then on pure impulse stood and ran after her. I heard Kim call for me, but ignored her. I caught up with Payton just outside the cafeteria, near the giant eagle mural. She was walking toward a dark haired, tan boy whom I recognized from my gym class last year; I never did learn his name. He was smiling as he watched her.

I recognized that look.

Payton walked up to him and grabbed his arm playfully, he handed her a book. I stopped and watched them walk away from me. It was hard to tell if there was anything besides friendship between the two, but the mere fact that there could be more, drove me crazy.

I spent the rest of the day replaying hundreds of scenarios in my head. I imagined myself walking up to them and grabbing Payton by the arm, telling her how I am dying inside not being able to talk to her and how I wanted nothing more than to make her happy. I also imagined beating up this, hard to admit, good looking stranger for the heck of it. However, every single one of my delusional dreams ended with Payton rejecting me while declaring that she would never be with somebody like me. Even my subconscious knew better than to let me think I stood a chance.

Instead of calling for Payton or running after her, I walked back to the lunchroom. The table closest to the double doors was empty except for a sad looking, short, blonde girl. I must have been too focused on chasing after Payton and had not seen her, somehow.

"Lynn? Are you okay?" I sat down next to her.

"I guess."

"Why are you sitting here by yourself?"

"Who else am I going to sit with?" she asked.

I didn't really know anyone to suggest, and I knew that I should have been more conscious of her. I wish I could just find her some good friends because I certainly didn't want her around the people I was associating with. Sometimes I felt like a complete hypocrite but, to be honest, I found it hard to focus on anything and could barely concentrate on what she was saying, because the truth of what I had just witnessed was sinking in. I had been discarded and replaced for a newer, less damaged model. Payton had invested in something broken, something that was beyond repair, *someone* whose worth had depreciated so much that the time spent in trying to repair it just wasn't worth it.

"Why did he do it? What was so important about you?" Lynn asked, dragging me from my self-deprecating thoughts.

I knew she didn't mean it condescendingly. She seemed genuinely confused; however, with the mood I was in, her words cut deep. *What was so important about me?*

"I don't know," I answered. "I really don't know."

"B.J. just seemed so nice and genuine,"

"I know, Lynn, but he was very deceptive," I said. I felt exhausted and my head was starting to ache.

"I was going to tell him that I didn't want to eat lunch with him anymore," Lynn's voice cracked, "but he never even showed up where we usually meet. I have no one, Jared. I am just so embarrassed. I can't believe I thought he might actually like me."

I felt the guilt. But justified it by telling myself I had done it for Lynn's own good. I had gotten rid of B.J. "You have me," I said happily. "Maybe I can help you find some new friends. At least now, without B.J. around, things will go back to normal."

"Normal? You say that like it's a good thing," Lynn said. "Going back to never having family dinner or never knowing anything about each other; seems like great fun to me." It wasn't hard to miss the sarcasm. "You know, I felt more like a family when B.J. was around, even if he was lying the entire time. He was very convincing though." Lynn said the last sentence so quietly, I almost didn't hear it.

"You're not the only one who fell for it."

"You didn't," she said sadly. "You never liked him."

"I know," was all I could say. It felt a little wrong taking credit for being such a good judge of character, but it wasn't hard to see that B.J. had been up to something.

"Was that girl the same one who wrote you those notes?" Lynn asked changing the subject.

I was confused.

"The one you were just chasing after?"

I nodded.

"You like her don't you?" she asked.

"Yes, I do."

"Well from the looks of it, it seems like we are in the same boat," Lynn said matter-of-factly. She started picking at her nail polish, and I knew she was trying to distract herself so she wouldn't start crying.

I paused and then mumbled, finishing her thought, “Liking someone who doesn’t like you back.”

Thirteen

I didn't feel seventeen.

I woke up to a warm March day, and stayed in bed as long as I could. I heard my dad ask my mom if she had picked up his suit from the dry cleaner and knew that he was packing to leave for California. I had mixed feelings. I didn't care to have him there on my birthday but I wondered if it bothered him at all to miss it.

"Who's ready for breakfast?" Lynn had announced proudly as she bounced into my room holding a tray filled with food.

"Wow," I sat up in bed. "Now that's what I call a breakfast." There were Eggs Benedict, bacon, and sausage pilled high on a plate. A fruit parfait was in a tiny glass bowl with a toasted bagel, smothered in cream cheese, lying next to it.

"I made it all myself!" Lynn said proudly. "Happy birthday!"

"I think you've found your calling in life," I said. I closed one eye suspiciously and asked, "Is my sister going to be the next Wolfgang Puck?"

Lynn giggled as she set the tray next to me on the bed. "Do you think I should take a cooking class for one of my electives next year, you know, to see if I would like being a chef?"

I put a forkful of eggs into my mouth and chewed slowly. I didn't answer until I had tasted a bite of everything on my plate. Lynn stuck her hand on her hip and tapped her foot, pretending like she was impatiently awaiting my answer. But she couldn't hide the smile that crept across her face every time I tried something new on my plate. I put my right hand up to my face and kissed my finger tips loudly, then dramatically opened my hand wide into the air, like an Italian would do after tasting something delicious. "I would eat at your restaurant every day!"

"You'd still have to pay," Lynn said as she pointed at me.

"What! How about a twenty percent discount?" I asked. "After all, I am your brother."

"Ten!"

I laughed, and then stuck a strip of bacon into my mouth. "Fine," I said, with my mouth full, "ten percent ... and only because your food tastes so good."

Lynn nodded her head once and then shook my hand. Before she left my room I said, "I would take as many cooking classes as I could if I were you."

"Okay." She smiled. "I'll come back in a little bit to see if you're done," Lynn said and then quickly added, "Oh, I almost forgot, Mom has a surprise for you."

"What ...," I started to ask, but Lynn just shook her head while running her pointer finger and thumb across her lips like she was zipping them shut, then left the room.

I had just finished my breakfast when someone lightly tapped on my door. "Come in," I yelled. I still hadn't gotten out of bed.

"Happy birthday, sweetie," my mom said as she sat down next to my feet. She paused and then awkwardly added, "Your father wanted me to tell you happy birthday for him ... he had to leave to catch his flight."

"Of course," I said. "We wouldn't want him missing his important business meeting."

My mom smiled sympathetically at me. "Your father just has a hard time expressing his emotions. But that doesn't mean he can't feel."

I knew that it was hard for my mom to defend him all the time and try to explain my dad's behavior. So instead of making a comment about how the only emotion I could ever evoke from him was rage and every other time he was more like a robot than my own father, I just said, "You know him better than I do."

Sadness flashed across my mom's face for a second before she pulled out a misshapen gift from her robe pocket. There was a red bow on top.

"You didn't have to get me anything," I said as I took the gift. It seemed that the older I got, the less I cared about getting things for my birthday. For Christmas every year I usually had already gotten everything I wanted or could possibly need, so when March eighteenth would come around it was hard for me to think of anything I wanted.

"It's nothing big," she said, her eyes sparkling a little. "I made them a couple of weeks ago."

"Made them?" Ever since my mom had quit her job, she has been experimenting with tole painting, scrapbooking, and as of late, sewing. My mom just smiled as I tore the blue wrapping paper, exposing two masks made of fabric.

"They're Batman and Robin masks," she said excitedly. Each mask had a band of elastic sewn to the sides. I chose the black Batman one, of course, and put it on.

"Thanks, they're great," I said as I took the mask back off and tried the light green and yellow one on.

"Don't you remember?" my mom asked, "when you were turning five, all you wanted for your birthday were Batman and Robin masks." My mom pointed to the masks I was holding. "We were desperate to find some, and had looked everywhere. Your father even called every store he could think of, but we never found them."

"I do remember," I said, remembering running around the house pretending to throw boomerangs while gliding through the air. I also remembered asking for a brother, every super hero needed a sidekick, but she didn't mention that.

"Do you like them? I know it's small and kind of childish ..."

"Like them? Mom I love them! You got me the one thing I had ever really wanted for my birthday," I interrupted.

"Twelve years late," she said smiling. "I just needed to take some time to actually learn to sew. But now a whole new world has been opened up to me."

"So?" I said, eyeing my mom, "next year can I get some capes?"

"I suppose so," she said laughing.

I put the masks on the nightstand by my bed and wondered how much time it had taken my mom to make them. "Thanks Mom. This was a great surprise; I have had a great birthday."

"Your birthday isn't over yet," my mom said, "unless you are planning on sleeping the rest of the day?" Her eyebrows rose as she questioned my plans for the next twelve hours or so.

I flopped back down on my pillow and put my hands behind my head. "Now that doesn't sound like a bad idea," I said. That way it would have been easier for me to sneak out of the house at one, and head to the marina for an hour at the most.

My mom smiled at me and then stood to leave. "It's your birthday, so you won't find me stopping you from sleeping the entire day away." Things seemed to be working out perfectly for me, besides the fact that I really wouldn't have minded bunkering down in my room the rest of the day instead of deceiving my family, yet again. "But I must tell you ... the masks weren't your surprise," my mom added, "this is!"

She had my full attention as she pulled out a decorative card from the same pocket where my gift had been. My name was written in cursive on top. My mom was beaming as I took it from her. "A sense of self-confidence and worth comes when you accept yourself as you are. Not when you're trying to be what other people expect," I read to myself. I could hear the blood rushing in my ears. My fingers started sweating where I was gripping the card as I read to myself, "Meet me on home plate at noon."

"You have an hour," my mom said as soon as I pried my eyes from the cursive black ink.

I gave her an accusatory look.

"I'm sorry ... I couldn't help myself," she said. "I found the card on our doorstep this morning." I really didn't care that she had snooped. I probably would have done the same thing. "So," my mom said slowly, "Is this the 'note girl'?" She looked as excited as I felt inside.

I read the note again.

"She's forgiven me," I said and then smiled, unable to suppress my cheesy grin any longer. *She gets me,* was all I kept thinking. I felt so relieved thinking that Payton had finally seen through my fake façade and found the real me. The "me" I now wanted to be. It was then that I realized that I would do anything for that girl. I would jump off a cliff for her ... completely sober.

I set the card next to my masks and then ran my fingers through my hair. "I should probably take a shower," I said as soon as I felt the clumps of day old hair gel.

"That would be a good idea," my mom said as she pinched her nose. She then quickly let go and placed her finger across her lips like she had just got an idea, and then said, "Oh ... and honey, wear your green and brown collared shirt, the one you got for Christmas. I think you look nice in it."

As my mom was leaving the room I jumped out of bed and caught her arm. "So, you think I should be getting ready to leave the house?" I asked, suddenly realizing that she had just given me permission to go out.

My mom placed her hand across my cheek and said, "Jared, you were such a good boy growing up," I dropped my head as a wave of guilt washed over me. "But now you are a man who has a good heart and is learning to be responsible. You deserve, on your birthday, to spend some time with a girl who see's in you, exactly what I do."

I didn't say anything, but my face must have said it all. "One day you better introduce me to this girl," my mom called over her shoulder as she left my room.

"Okay, sure." My mom had never met anyone I had ever dated before. I had mentioned Kim's name on occasion and Kim had introduced herself to my mom at a softball game last year, but that was the extent of it. I actually kind of liked the idea of bringing Payton to the house; I knew that my mom would instantly love her.

I wondered if I was getting too ahead of myself when I realized I couldn't stop smiling. I chose to be optimistic as I stripped off my shirt and then grabbed my phone. I left Derek a text message rather than calling him. That way I wouldn't have to hear him beg when I told him that my plans had changed and I wouldn't make it to the lake.

ಬ

I pulled into the stall closest to the baseball field and from the driver's seat of my car I could see the top of a brunette's head between the slits in the aluminum bleachers. I couldn't remember feeling that disappointed in a long time. I sat in my car for a bit, wondering if I should just leave. It wasn't hard to figure out who was waiting for me. She was still waiting for my answer. I went there too willingly, even excitedly, thinking that it was Payton wanting to meet me instead of Kim. She didn't deserve that, and I needed to make her move on. I took a deep breath and met her on home plate.

"Hey, birthday boy!" Kim called, and then ran to meet me at the gate. She paused in front of me for a second, and then as if deciding to be forward, wrapped her arms tightly around my neck.

I ended the embrace almost as soon as it began. I hated doing that to her, but I needed to do this for both of our sakes. I didn't have the same feelings as she had for me. I needed to stop confusing her with my mixed signals. "Thanks," was all I could think to say. She had distanced herself from me considerably and had her arms folded protectively against her.

It wasn't until then that I noticed the gift bag sitting on the ground. Kim followed my gaze and said quietly, "Oh, it's just something stupid."

Things were starting to become excruciatingly painful and I didn't help the hurt when I said, "I thought you were going to be someone else." I was having a staring competition with home plate because I was a coward and couldn't look her in the eyes.

"I know," she said sadly, and then added, "remember last week when you were reading that note before class?"

"Yes," I knew what she was getting at.

"I may have seen what was written before you shoved it into your pocket," her voice lowered to a whisper, "and it didn't take a rocket scientist to figure out who the note was from."

"If you knew ... then why would you leave this?" I held up the card she had left on my doorstep.

Kim started to tear up. "I knew it was the only way you would come for sure ... and I guess I needed to see for myself if you would be disappointed." Kim wiped her eyes feverishly and then attempted to smile. "I got my answer."

She stopped me from saying anything and then pulled her cell phone from her pocket, "You have fifteen minutes to get to the lake for your party. You owe it to Derek to show up," she said pointing at me, "and you're welcome for getting you out of the house without having to sneak and deceive your family."

"Does Derek know about this?"

"Yes, I told him I was going to be with you and that I would get you to the lake on time."

I now understood why Derek hadn't texted me back or tried to call me at all after I cancelled on him. I felt betrayed but was having a hard time focusing on myself when I could visibly see what I had done to Kim. I wanted nothing more than to spend the day with Payton but wanted to physically slap myself for thinking that she would ever forgive me and go as far as wanting to meet and spend time with me.

"Okay," I said submissively.

"I'll let Derek know that you are on your way."

"Aren't you coming?" I asked.

"I was, but now I think I am just going to go home." Kim walked away from me toward the grassy outfield. I saw her car parked on the road which ran along the outfield fence, partially concealed behind an old tree.

"Enjoy," Kim said to me as she pointed to the gift sitting on home plate.

"Kim, I'm sorry," I stammered, unsure what to say or do.

"Don't worry," Kim bit her bottom lip, "I knew it was coming. I just hoped you would have changed your mind."

It was a windless warm afternoon and I was sweating, I believe more from the pressure I had felt turning Kim down than the weather. Things were becoming awkward as we stood there. "So, uh ... do you want a ride to the lake? I mean, we can go together. There's no reason for you to miss it." I finally said.

"No thanks," Kim said and then pointed to her car, "I may make it to the party at Bobby's tonight, that is if ...," she paused for a second and then cocked her head. "Are you going to be at the party tonight?"

"No, I wasn't planning on going."

"Well then in that case, I will probably go to that party then." She laughed.

I laughed with her. I was impressed with the way she was handling everything and couldn't help but notice how pretty she looked. I felt that I owed her more, more of an apology, or maybe more of an explanation. Before I could think of something else to add she said, "Well I am going to go before you start telling me how special I am and how I will find somebody else."

"I was going to say that there are plenty of other fish in the sea," I said matching her light tone.

Kim smiled and then took three quick steps toward me. She hugged me and then quickly said, "Not to me." Kim let go and looked at me then said in a husky voice, "I just lost a one of a kind fish." She kissed me on the cheek and then left.

I waited until she had driven away before picking up the gift bag. It felt wrong to take it, but I didn't want to leave it there. I opened it once I was in my car. Kim had framed the picture she had taken of us at the party. I was smiling as Kim was kissing me, Derek was in the background his mouth wide open and tongue sticking out. Below our faces was a quote from Dr. Seuss, "Be who you are and say what you feel, because those who mind don't matter and those who matter don't mind."

I wondered if Kim was confused with "who I was," or at least who I wished I was. Determining that was the ultimate goal because it is only then that I would be able to tell who mattered and who didn't.

&

I frantically searched the murky water. I could barely see my hand in front of me. Deciding to switch my tactics I swam deeper waving my arms and feet, trying to feel for anything, hoping to feel something. My lungs were burning, I grasped at the dark space in front of me, there was nothing. I started to feel light headed and my fingers were tingling. I had to turn around. Once my face broke the surface I gasped for air. Even the water in my ears couldn't dull the screaming and yelling.

"I think she's over there," I heard a girl scream shrilly.

"Keep looking!" someone else yelled.

"There!" I heard Derek yell, "Bubbles! I saw bubbles over there!"

"Directions!" I screamed as I treaded water, "I can't see where you are pointing."

"Swim closer to the boat," Derek said. Once I swam a few feet he yelled, "Stop! Right there ... I saw them right there." His voice broke and just as I took a deep breath I think I heard him say, "Hurry, she is going to die." I heard it so clearly that I'm still not sure if it was all in my head, if I had said it to myself, urging me to try harder, move faster.

I swept my arms all around me as I swam deeper and deeper. The deeper I swam the harder I prayed. I remembered reading that if the Lake were completely full it would reach a depth of five hundred feet.

I started to panic.

I was a decent swimmer but knew that I had limits. I was torn, either I left her there to die or else we both would die. I tried praying one last time, "Help me," was all I said. I moaned as I flipped around, intending to swim back up for air. Instantly, that uncomfortable yet familiar electric feeling started flooding the top of my head, it quickly spread to my face, as I floated closer to the surface.

I screamed losing the rest of the air I had been storing in my lungs.

I couldn't see anything or more accurately, anyone. I imagined the horror of B.J. finding me in this wet grave to exact his revenge. The electricity seemed worse underwater. I could barely stand it, and the more I floated to the surface the more it burned. I waved my arms desperately trying to sink deeper, I would have done anything to get rid of the pain, even drown.

The pain left my face, and was running up my forehead to the top of my head. I thrust myself deeper in one last weak effort, when a clump of hair tangled around my fingers. The pain and electric intensity immediately stopped. I quickly closed my hand into a fist and yanked hard until I could get my arm around her waist. She wasn't moving at all, so it was twice as hard getting to the boat.

It seemed like I was swimming forever, I needed oxygen, and worried that I was slowing down. My mind was racing and I tried to think of anything to keep me from losing it. I thought about how I had arrived at the marina just twenty minutes earlier and never expected to be swimming for my life and someone else's.

"We've been waiting for you," Derek had yelled from his family's white Cabin Cruiser when I had stepped out of my car. He was wearing an eye patch and a pirate's hat. I had been on his boat once before. It had a small kitchen area, toilet and a place for two people to sleep. It was about thirty feet in length and had enough room for the ten or so people I saw on it. "Where's Kim?"

"She's not coming, but she did mention she would make it to the party tonight."

"You broke her heart, didn't you?" Derek had said. He made a clicking sound with his mouth. He jumped from the side of the boat onto the dock. "Happy birthday," he said as he bumped my fist.

"Thanks ... I didn't want to, but needed to stop lying to myself and her."

"You're going to regret it; that's all I have to say." Derek had watched me for a while and then added, "But that's the last thing I am going to say about the subject. Just don't come crying to me when someone else snags her."

"Okay," I said.

"It's time to hoist anchor mateys, Jared is here," Derek yelled.

"Where's your dad?" I asked. I knew that Derek hadn't towed the boat out there on his own and the last time we had gone out on the lake, Steve, his dad, had taken us out.

"He just left to get some lunch, or maybe a beer, who knows. He said that I could take 'Darlene' out on the water whenever I wanted."

"Darlene?"

"An old girlfriend that he must have been fond of, I guess. My mom refuses to go out on the lake in it, which is probably why he won't ever change the name."

I started to recognize a few people the closer we got to the boat, but there were still some I swore I had never seen in my life.

"Happy birthday, All-star!" Gus had called from the boat. He was lounged across the back of the boat on a large beach towel. One of the girls I didn't know was wrapped around him. "Derek keeps his promises," he said pointing dramatically to the red head lying next to him.

"Derek," one of Derek's girls from the party he had thrown last weekend whined, "I want you ... you need to help me put sun some block on." She started giggling uncontrollably and then said slowly, "I mean some sun block on."

"Which one is she?"

"Brandi," Derek answered. "And we may have taste tested some of the beverages that will be served at tonight's party before we got here." Brandi was leaning far over the railing holding a bottle of sun tan lotion. A guy named Justin, had run up behind her and grabbed a hold of her shirt so she wouldn't fall over.

Five minutes later Derek had untied the boat and we were heading toward the middle of the lake. Once we had stopped at a place that Derek thought would be good for swimming, everything seemed to have happened so fast. I was taking off my shirt when I heard a girl scream. I made my way to where Derek and a group of people were standing. They were looking over the side of the boat.

"I was trying to get her to stop, but she was leaning so far over the railing," Derek rambled, his face was white.

"She hit her head on the side of the boat when she fell," her friend Amanda had said frantically. "She was probably knocked out." Everyone seemed to be standing there, doing nothing, just staring into the water. I had pushed my way through the crowd and without thinking dove head first into the water.

It seemed like an eternity since I had jumped into the water, but I knew that only a few minutes had passed. I could see the light shining through the water and knew that I was seconds away from breathing in fresh air. I tightened my grip around Brandi's waist. I breathed in greedily as soon as I had reached the surface. My lips tingled from a lack of oxygen.

Once both of us were hoisted out of the water and into the boat, I wonder if I went into shock, because everything seemed hazy like I was in a daze. I laid there on the boat's floor and could hear several girls sobbing. Someone was panicking and pacing back and forth, he cursed and then said, "What do we do? We need to call someone."

Derek came over to me and grabbed both of my shoulders, "She isn't breathing, Jared," he said.

I sat up abruptly and a wave of nausea hit me. I had swallowed a lot of water and was feeling sick. I crawled over to the girl and pushed everyone I could reach aside, bent down next to her and grabbed her wrist. The second I didn't feel a pulse I started chest compressions. I had never performed CPR on a live person before, but it wasn't a lot different than the dummies we had to practice on during certification. I pumped exactly thirty times then tilted her chin up, covered her mouth with mine, and gave her two quick breaths.

I repeated this three times, and when I was starting my fourth round of chest compressions, a gurgling sound came from Brandi's mouth. I quickly tilted her on her side as she coughed up water. She then started gasping for air and seemed to be breathing fine on her own. Her friend Amanda quickly wrapped her in a towel and several guys carried her to the bed inside the boat. I collapsed right where I had been kneeling as Derek raced the boat to the dock.

"What's going on?" I heard Steve, Derek's dad, yell from shore.

"We need to call an ambulance," Amanda yelled, "my friend nearly drowned."

The sun was beating down on my face, I felt completely exhausted. To this day, I still don't know how I mustered the strength to resuscitate that girl.

"What? Are you kidding me?" Derek's dad said. I then could hear him telling someone our location and the description of the boat.

"Jared! Let's get you up." I opened my eyes and Derek was standing over me. I felt groggy like I had fallen asleep.

I let him help me off the boat. Everyone was standing on the shore. Brandi was sitting on the tailgate of Derek's truck with a towel wrapped tightly around her. A few people still looked shaken up but for the most part everyone seemed to be recovering from the ordeal.

Within minutes a ranger patrol boat had pulled up and docked next to us. A skinny man with a mustache wearing a ranger's uniform walked toward us and before he could open his mouth to ask a single question we started to hear sirens that were steadily getting louder. An ambulance and a police car turned into the parking lot and drove to where we were all standing.

Paramedics started inspecting Brandi and eventually loaded her onto a gurney and were getting ready to roll her into the back of the ambulance.

"Why are you taking her? Is she going to be all right?" Amanda asked.

"She seems fine. This is just a precaution that we need to take," said one of the paramedics.

Amanda came up to both Derek and me who were getting ready to be questioned by the police officer whose name was

Officer Roosendaal. “I am going to leave so I can be at the hospital when Brandi and her parents arrive,” she said.

“Ma’am, I need to get your contact information so that if we have any questions we can call you.” Amanda looked at us nervously but then wrote down her information on the notepad the officer had handed her.

Derek and I were questioned for at least ten minutes. We both recounted every detail that had happened that day accurately, although we both neglected to inform the officer of the drinking Derek and the girls had been doing before the party. However I didn’t doubt that there was a possibility that the truth would surface.

I heard Derek’s dad tell Officer Roosendaal’s partner that he had been on shore the entire time. And both Gus and another guy interjected that they had helped locate the girl in the water.

“Man, I was freaking out for a second,” Derek whispered to me when the cop car pulled out of the marina parking lot. “I was sure they were going to find out I had been drinking.”

“They still may find out,” I said shaking my head. I couldn’t believe Derek was more worried about getting caught than if Brandi were okay.

“How?”

“At this very moment Brandi is most likely getting tons of tests done at the hospital. And you don’t think that one of those tests will show her blood alcohol level?” I was starting to get angry. “And how confident are you that your name won’t come up?”

My tone must have struck a nerve because Derek shot back, “Now don’t get all high and mighty on me now,” He dug a finger into my chest, “over some lame class project.”

I was getting sick of Derek analyzing my behavior and saying that I was changing for some school assignment. “Maybe I am just realizing that I am better than all this,” I shot back as I waved my arms acknowledging everyone around me who had stopped talking to one another to hear the conversation Derek and I were having.

“Just a week ago you were right with us, partying hard, acting recklessly, breaking the rules,” Derek said mockingly. He shook his pointer finger at me and dramatically covered his opened mouth with his other hand. Gus and a few others laughed.

Their laughter fueled Derek's fire. "You even had a beautiful brunette practically throwing herself at you ... but now you're what, some kind of priest? Too good to hang out with us?" he sneered.

I took a few deep breaths. I didn't want to lose my temper. Once I had felt myself relax a little I happened to notice Derek's dad turn around and walk back to his car, he must have no longer felt that a fight was going to break out.

"I just can't believe that after everything that has happened, you still plan on partying some more tonight," I said calmly.

"You may have forgotten, but all of this *was* for you!"

"No, it's not!" I laughed out loud. "It's so you can have an excuse to get some girls drunk."

Anger flashed in Derek's eyes. "Well ... since one of mine is indisposed at the moment how about I trade her in for another young, impressionable, naïve freshman." Derek leaned in closer to me and said cockily, "You know without those glasses Lynn could be pretty hot."

That was when I punched him in the face.

Fourteen

"By the time someone enters the preparation stage, the pros in favor of making a change greatly outweigh the cons." Mrs. Flint said to the class as she placed the number fourteen manila envelope on my desk and walked away. Several students were reading the messages from their partners and some had even started writing. They were most likely deciding a form of action to take to make their "change" and hoping to get some feedback. I left my folder unopened for most of the class period.

Just being in that class felt like a battleground; I was completely surrounded. Enemies were on all sides of me. All I wanted was an ally. I think Payton probably noticed a change in Derek's, Kim's and my dynamic, but not enough to speak to me.

Actually everyone in the class probably noticed the change in our relationship. If we weren't in school I am pretty sure Derek would have tried to smash my face like I had done to him two days ago. He was fuming in his seat, so much so, that I wouldn't have been surprised to see him spontaneously combust right there in the middle of psychology class.

Kim had avoided looking at me when I walked into the room, probably to keep from talking to me. She was trying to act strong and indifferent, but for the most part she just looked sad. She had caught my eye briefly when Mr. Atwood announced over the school's loud speaker that Brandi Banovich had been involved in a boating accident over the weekend. Mr. Atwood explained that Brandi had recently been released from the hospital and was now resting comfortably at home. I could hear Derek grind his teeth the entire time the announcement was made. "We will also be having a mandatory assembly during fourth period, about the dangers of drinking," Mr. Atwood continued to say.

I started to chuckle, pointed at Derek and said, "What did I tell you." Derek breathed out heavily without glancing at me.

"I don't think what happened is a laughing matter," Payton whispered in my ear from behind me.

I cringed.

I could only imagine what she was thinking about me. My only thought was that at that exact moment she probably was comparing me to that other guy she had been with. She was probably thinking that he wouldn't have joked about something this serious. I at least hoped she could see the tension between Derek and me. However, her comment indicated that she pegged me just as responsible for Brandi's accident as anyone else who was at that party.

I couldn't help but keep making mistakes when it came to Payton. Even when I was trying to change and do better, I was failing in her eyes. I knew how both Kim and Derek would react to hearing my inner thoughts, but I still wanted to make myself acceptable in Payton's eyes.

"I don't either," I said louder than she had and then purposely looked at both Kim and Derek. Payton didn't say anything else and I could hear her unzip her backpack and put papers into it. I decided to open my envelope. I needed a distraction.

My partner had written a small message to me on the top of a lined piece of paper that asked, "What do you want your future to be like?"

I wasn't sure.

I just didn't want to have to look back at my life only to find a million regrets. "I don't know. I just picked something that I thought would get me a good grade," I wrote on the next line under the question. Only to erase it and write, "I want to be rich, and date a model."

Half way down the lined paper, my partner had a list of three goals to help "change someone's life." This person is so egotistical, I thought, before I started reading the goals. "Learn to be a good friend," was written after the first bullet point. "Try to be a good example to them," was the second, and "convince them that they can change their future," was the last thing written.

I couldn't believe it, this person was turning the assignment into some "intervention" and I was the subject. I slammed the paper down on my desk.

"Having a hard time deciding which friend to betray next, Saint Jared?" Derek asked. He didn't look up but kept doodling inappropriate cartoons all over his paper.

I looked back down at what I had written, and then erased my answer once again. I didn't want to be like Derek, even if that meant I had to deal with my partner's approach to the assignment. I was once again thankful for the anonymity of this project.

"I don't know for sure, but I think I want to have a better relationship with my family. I want to have no regrets, and I want to be known as a good person." I quickly wrote down on the paper and shoved it back into the envelope before I could change my mind.

ꝏ

I walked through the parking lot to my car. I was surprised to find the passenger door unlocked, Lynn must have forgotten again. I reclined the seat back and popped a potato chip into my mouth. On my way out of the cafeteria I had stopped at a vending machine to buy a bag of chips and a Gatorade.

Before I had gotten to my car, things had not gone well. "Look everyone, it's our old friend ... the one who's too good for us now," Derek had said as I walked past their table to the wall with the vending machines. Derek was the only one doing the talking. Gus dropped his head and acted like he was busy eating. Kim watched me. She had looked torn, as I walked away.

Once I grabbed my food, it had only taken a quick glance around the room to realize that I had nowhere to go. I didn't belong anywhere. It seemed that more than a few people were watching me, and I couldn't wait to get out of there. That was one of the few times I had ever truly felt alone.

There were a few stray skittles floating around my feet, so I went to throw them out my window when I noticed Lynn walking toward the car. As soon as she saw me she stopped. She was holding a brown paper sack.

"Hey," I called out the window.

She starting walking to the car again, and once she was close enough she stammered, "I uh, think I left one of my books in your car."

I smiled and said, "Feel free to look around," knowing that there wasn't a single book in my car. I now knew why my door had been unlocked. She probably intentionally did it so that she could also have a safe place to eat her lunch. I wondered how many times she had eaten in my car alone.

Lynn stood outside the door and quickly looked through the back passenger side window, "I don't see it." She bit her lip and then looked back at the school building.

"Sorry about your book," I said. "But since you are here, would you like to join me?"

"Sure," she said excitedly as she climbed into the back seat. She smiled at me and then added shyly, "Um, you have friends ... so, uh, why are you eating out here?"

"I don't anymore." I popped another chip into my mouth and Lynn watched me out of the corner of her eye for just a moment and then pulled a sandwich and an apple from the paper sack. It looked like she had decided to let it go, something I was grateful for.

"I saw B.J. today," Lynn said quietly. "He wanted to make sure I had someone to eat with." Lynn paused and then added, "I told him that I was going to be with you, thinking that I would just tell a lie to make him feel better, but I guess it ended up being the truth."

"I guess so," I said. "And isn't your brother better company?" I grinned widely at her, showing my teeth.

Lynn giggled. "We may not have friends, but we have each other."

We had a peaceful thirty minutes of eating and some small talk. Lynn seemed to thrive from the social interaction. I wished lunch would have lasted longer than an hour. I needed more times like that with my sister, and I think she did too.

"So I'll see you again tomorrow, same place and time?" I said.

Lynn's face brightened. "And next time ... I'll pack you a lunch."

ꕥ

"I just don't get it bro," Derek said in between breaths. "Who do you have now?" he asked. I was leading our teams run and he had sprinted ahead to catch up to me. "From the looks of things this morning, I'd guess you don't have Payton's friendship. You've made it clear that you don't want mine or Kim's," Derek was breathing deeply as he tried to match my pace, "I'm just curious about who you have now?"

I continued to look forward and even lengthened my stride slightly, my lungs felt like they were on fire. My body was still feeling the effects of my near drowning experience. I kept replaying in my mind the image of me socking Derek in the nose. It helped keep me from doing it again.

"Do you also disapprove of Gus, and his choices?" Derek asked mockingly as he nodded to the rest of the team following behind us who were well within ear shot of our conversation.

"Keep me out of it," I heard Gus say in a hoarse voice. We had three more laps around the baseball diamond before we were done and Gus didn't sound like he was going to make it.

"Or, what about the rest of your team, I mean; there were a lot who showed up to your party." Derek smiled broadly at me. "You know ... the one you didn't come to." Derek turned completely around and started jogging backward as he said loudly, "Are you also too good for them and the choices they make? Team Captain!"

"Give it a rest," I heard someone say.

"No, he probably thinks he's too good to play ball with us, too," said another person.

"Do you feel that way?" Derek asked.

I looked over and Derek had slowed down slightly so he was running alongside B.J. I had forgotten he was even there. Ironically it seemed that I had other problems that seemed more intense than all the issues I had with B.J.

"Do you feel like Jared thinks he's better than you?" Derek asked. B.J. looked up at me. Sweat was pouring down his forehead.

He didn't answer Derek.

"Because he thinks he's better than you! I wish you could have heard all the stuff he was saying about you last week." Derek shook his head and then said, "It wasn't right ... but I defended you."

I quickly looked away. It felt cowardly. My aversion toward B.J. hadn't eased at all but I didn't like the implication that I was tiptoeing around his back, talking smack. He didn't make a sound when Derek said, "I wish I would have invited you to this fool's party. It would have been hilarious to see Jared's face as soon as he noticed you there." Derek laughed out loud at himself. He was still jogging backward and was having a hard time keeping his footing. He almost fell when he had stepped on a small hole in the grass.

"You can be the new and improved version," Derek said. I turned and he was pointing at B.J., who was still watching me. "How about that guys," Derek raised his voice, "B.J.'s just as good as Jared, let's have him lead our team. And this way, our team's leader won't sell out on us and go soft."

B.J. started shaking his head slowly. "Hang with me and you can have it all ... girls ... booze ... popularity ... girls," Derek said quietly. "What do you say?"

We only had half a lap to go. I could pick up the pace even more and hopefully this conversation would be forced to end, especially with Coach Kline within earshot, but instead I slowed down. I knew that Derek had no authority to appoint a new team captain, but I was interested in hearing B.J.'s answer. If he were to be linked with Derek, I would be rid of him. There would be little chance of him slipping his way back into mine or my family's life.

"Did you not hear anything that Mr. Atwood said at the assembly?" Gus asked breathlessly.

"I had another pressing matter," Derek said.

"Meeting up with Amanda on the side of the gym?" asked Gus.

"Precisely."

I breathed out loudly.

"Oh, so you disapprove Saint Jared?"

I sure did.

"So, are you just going to ignore me?" Derek asked. I didn't look at him but was pretty sure he was talking to me. B.J. still hadn't answered him though.

"You didn't miss much," Gus interjected, sounding horrible. "Underage drinking is bad. Don't do it. Find a hobby you enjoy. Talk to your parents more. Have good friends," Gus said in a deep monotone, breathless voice. He actually sounded a lot like Mr. Atwood.

I had sat through the assembly that afternoon. It was more of a lecture than anything. A lot of facts were read. Though it was a boring presentation, the information made sense.

"Well, I don't need you to talk to me." Derek sounded angry, but it could also have been because he was struggling talking after nine laps. "I have the new and improved version right here." I turned to see that Derek had flipped around and was running alongside B.J., his arm was around his shoulder. It looked awkward because both of them were panting and trying to keep their balance.

"I'll make you a deal, you teach me how to hit the ball out of the park and I'll be your mentor with everything else."

There was a short pause. I couldn't look away. I was too curious.

"No, thanks," B.J. said quietly.

Derek tightened his arm around B.J.'s shoulders aggressively. "You must not fully understand the opportunity I am giving you."

I was shocked when I felt a tinge of respect for B.J.'s decision.

Before Derek could try to intimidate B.J. any further, B.J. flipped Derek's arm off and said crisply, "I do understand the opportunity and am not interested." B.J. caught my eye. I looked away, once again.

"Why?" Derek asked rudely.

"Because I'd rather be alone than follow you."

It was silent besides a few snickers. I wanted to laugh out loud, and would have if it were anybody else but B.J.

"Is anyone else hearing this?" Derek yelled loudly. He was jogging backward again. "B.J. would rather be alone."

"Yep," B.J. said briskly.

"That can be arranged," Derek said more quietly. "You can join Jared and have nobody. Forever alone, that's what you two are."

The hole in the grass was coming up again, and we only had a few more yards to run before practice was over. Derek was going to miss it completely. I started to subtly shift to the right. "Forever alone," I heard Derek say again. I cut even more sharply to the right. The team followed me without question, that is, if they even noticed our course had changed slightly. Everyone was exhausted. The hole was approaching quickly and I knew it was a long shot. Even if I could get him close enough to the hole, he could easily just run right over it, missing it completely. I continued to veer to the right, in one last ditch effort to get Derek as close to it as possible.

I looked behind me just as I had passed the hole. It was only a few more seconds before Derek would get to it, but it looked like he was still a little too far to the left. B.J. was even farther to the left but I watched as he quickly cut the distance between Derek and him. I couldn't tell if he were just trying to follow my course or if he was also intending for Derek to trip. B.J. pressed even closer to Derek. Derek glared at B.J. and then shoved off of him, yelling, "Get away from me loser!" just as his left foot disappeared into the grass.

He fell right on his face.

It had just struck me as funny, watching Derek eat dirt. Tears instantly sprang to my eyes even before I had ever started laughing. Everyone circled around Derek who was still lying flat on his stomach. We were just a few yards from the infield. Most of the team was laughing now, B.J. just smiled. I tried to catch a breath, from the running and now laughing, I felt light headed.

"It's good to see your mouth has other uses," I choked out. I was laughing so hard I was wheezing. Derek lifted his chest off the ground, spit out a mouthful of grass, and then charged me.

"Jared! Derek! I need to talk to you two, right now!" Coach Kline yelled from the dugout; his face was red and splotchy. Derek had barreled into me knocking me onto my back. He had only gotten one good hit on me and my left jaw was throbbing. I underestimated how angry he was. Coach Kline stopped the fight before I could retaliate.

As soon as we were within a few feet of him he excused both the assistant coach and trainer, saying that he needed a few minutes alone with Derek and me. Coach was always good at bringing out the fear in people when necessary. And I was afraid.

Coach Kline told us to sit on the wooden bench in the dugout. He placed an overturned bucket near us, which he usually kept the team's baseballs in, and sat on it. We had been having a mediocre practice at best and the tension between my old friend and me wasn't helping.

"Do either one of you have any idea what is happening this Thursday?" Without a second delay, and obviously not wanting a response, he answered, "It's our first game of the season!" He stared both of us down, his eye started to twitch. "Does that mean anything to either one of you?"

"Yes, I know that we ...," I began to say, before he abruptly stood up and kicked the bucket sending it crashing into the chain link fence.

He pointed his finger threateningly at my face, "Don't speak," he managed to say. "I expected more from you Jared. Is this the way a team captain should behave?"

I didn't dare answer.

I could see Derek's expression change from fear to smugness. "Nope," Derek barely whispered. That was when Coach Kline turned on him.

He got in Derek's face and screamed, "Your place on this team is barely hanging by a thread, and it is fraying quickly!"

"Yes, sir."

"I saw what you were doing out there a couple minutes ago. Y'all must think I have marbles for brains!" He pointed to his head. "Get out of here," he shooed Derek away with the wave of his hand. "You aren't worth the trouble."

Derek slowly stood and walked out of the dugout. He looked confused and I wondered if he also wasn't sure if he were still on the team or not. This fact made my heart quicken.

Derek had almost made it to the outer gate where the rest of the team was packing up. He watched us nervously, until Coach yelled, "Derek! If you so much as breathe wrong, you might as well kiss high school baseball goodbye!"

Derek started nodding his head enthusiastically. "I hear you Coach. You don't need to worry about me." He almost started skipping as he ran to catch up to Gus who was loading his bat bag into the bed of his old blue Dodge Ram.

The fact that Derek still had a spot on the team, made my heart rate slow slightly. The chances of me being kicked out over Derek were minuscule. I still felt disappointed though.

"What is going on?" Coach asked, after he had grabbed the overturned bucket. He genuinely sounded baffled.

"I ... I don't know," I lied. "Things have just been off between Derek and me."

I knew Coach wasn't buying it but was shocked to see a little sadness in his face. I wondered if he felt I should be able to confide in him, at least better than I was.

"I get it," he said quietly, "You aren't going to tell me a thing."

When I heard that, I almost blurted out everything, how I had no friends anymore, how I was tired of being a fake person, how a majority of my teammates were now almost enemies to me. Luckily I stopped because he finally said, "Actually ... it's probably better I don't know. I want you two to either fix it, and if that doesn't work, you better both be really good actors. Do you get my drift?"

"Yes Coach, I do."

"We play our first season game Thursday, and we are going to need all the teamwork we can get."

Fifteen

"Uh," my dad cleared his throat, "Did uh, you have a good ... weekend."

I didn't turn around. I was so close to killing the last zombie on level nine, and I didn't want to talk to him.

"I asked you a question, son."

I shot the last decrepit creature a record number of times before flipping the control onto the couch next to me. I looked up at my dad who was standing behind the sofa. His tie was undone, so that meant he was coming home. My mom was making spaghetti in the kitchen and announced, "Dinner is ready, wash up."

I tried to walk past my dad to the kitchen, but he had blocked my path, he stared intently at me, breathing deep, angry breaths.

I smiled big and put a hand across my chest, "It was magical ... the best weekend of my entire life."

My dad spun on his heels, and walked away. A few seconds later I heard his door slam shut. My mom stared at the floor for a while and then finished helping my grandpa get something to drink. She then started dishing up a plate of spaghetti, salad, and breadsticks. She called for Lynn. "Sweetie can you bring a dinner plate to your father?"

When Lynn didn't respond, she briefly looked at me and then straightened her apron, plastered one of her fake smiles onto her face and walked the plate to the master bedroom. I didn't wait for anyone as I splattered a large helping of spaghetti onto my plate. I grabbed a piece of garlic bread and used it to shovel the noodles into my mouth. I didn't even bother using a fork. I was half way through with my meal when Lynn walked into the kitchen.

She was wearing flannel pajama pants and one of my old tee shirts. Even with the way she looked, I noticed how much she had grown up. It was weird how just a month can change you. The only thing she was missing was a smile.

"Are you all right?" I asked. She quietly grabbed a plate and a fork. Her back was to me, but I could see her shoulders start shaking.

I set my plate down and walked behind her and slowly turned her around. She looked up at me and couldn't hold it in any longer. Lynn buried her head into my chest. "I hate my life," she sobbed.

I tried to pry her away, so I could see her face and talk some sense into her. She finally gave in, letting me hold her by both arms a few inches from me. "What are you talking about? What happened?"

"I'm just not one of those girls."

"Who? What girls are we talking about?" I felt lost and wondered if I shouldn't have been.

"No girl in particular, just the kind that catches all the breaks," she clarified.

"Oh, that kind."

Lynn started to smile and I could see her relax a little. I think she could see I was struggling. I grabbed her plate and started to get her some food.

"In my last class today, Lindsey, you know ... the girl who used to be my friend," Lynn said.

"Yeah, yeah I know who she is," I answered quickly, hoping that bringing her up wouldn't make Lynn even more upset.

"Well ... she got asked to prom."

I had finished pouring strawberry vinaigrette on top of her colorless salad. I was expecting something more, something more traumatic.

"And ... that's bad," I said definitively, even though I meant it more as a question.

"Exactly!" she shouted. Lynn pointed to me dramatically, "He gets it! And he has a 'y' chromosome. Why don't the other boys understand this?"

I shrugged my shoulders and said, "Beats me." I laughed to myself at the irony of my statement. Then Lynn got serious, her eyebrows pierced together.

"Doug, a boy in my class, said something about how only the hot freshmen get asked to prom and then he said that I shouldn't get my hopes up. Everyone laughed." she said and then grabbed a napkin off the counter and held it to her face.

"Doug who?!" I said loudly.

"It doesn't matter Jared. What matters, is that he is right."

"What if I told you that I don't believe that ... and that I would be completely shocked if you didn't get asked," I said more quietly.

"I would say that you are the only one." Lynn's sad eyes stared at me, then a smile crept into them when she added, "You're a good brother." I smiled back and handed her the plate. She grabbed a handful of cherry tomatoes and plopped them on top of her salad.

I was rinsing off my plate at the sink when my mom finally came out of my parents' room. She was holding her folded apron, walked past Lynn and me and hung it up on a hook by the refrigerator. Her eyes were puffy. And like always I didn't know what to say or do.

"Mom," Lynn said. My mom looked at her, but I'm not sure if she actually saw her. "Would you like me to fix you a plate?"

"No, honey, I'm not really hungry. I think I am going to go for a drive."

I wanted to scream. The plate I was holding was shaking violently. I wanted to crush it with my bare hands. I didn't have the nerve to ask if her change in mood was because of me. I just knew that he was taking his anger out on her. But even if I asked, she wouldn't have told the truth.

"Please just make sure your grandfather get's enough to eat," my mom said quietly. "And then Lynn, can you make sure he gets downstairs safely?"

Lynn nodded.

After we had all eaten, Lynn made sure that grandpa was comfortable downstairs in his chair. We put all the left-over food into containers and washed the pans, without saying anything to each other. She must have been too caught up in her own thoughts, like me.

Dinner had been depressing, but it was hard remembering our meals ending any other way, especially lately. I could remember having a happy childhood, at least I remembered being happy, I thought. Things seemed to be getting progressively worse, and I knew the part I was playing in it. I just didn't know how to stop.

By the end of that school year, according to Mrs. Flint, I was supposed to have experienced my change. I felt so strongly that there was no possible way that in just a few short months, I would have a better relationship with my dad. I had so many regrets and felt that they weren't going anywhere, just following me through life, continually growing as I made mistakes. And even though Lynn had said earlier that evening that I was a "good brother," I feared that I still wasn't a good person.

An hour had passed since my mom had left. I threw on some baggy sweat pants and a sweatshirt. I opened Lynn's bedroom door and said, "Hey, I'm going to go for a run, and maybe see if I can find where mom went."

Lynn was on her laptop. She looked up and said, "Mom's at the ..."

"I know," I interrupted quickly. Lynn nodded and then focused her attention back on the colored screen.

༄

My Mom's grey Sonata was the only car in the parking lot. Exactly where I knew I would find it. Most of the street lamps' bulbs were out, casting an eerie glow.

I hated being there.

I didn't have to look to know that just beyond the clump of pine trees and down the small paved road; I would find her, sitting in front of his headstone. When I was younger we used to often go there as a family. Now only she went.

I wanted to give my mom privacy but wanted to make sure she was safe. So without her noticing I crossed Adams Boulevard, before disappearing onto a connecting road. It was nice outside and I liked having the chance to think. I let my mind run wild as I randomly wound my way through the city's streets. I could tell that it was getting late because most of the homes I jogged past were dark.

I turned right onto a street that's sign was blocked by a giant hedge but knew that it most likely connected with Arizona Street, which I could follow all the way home.

I noticed an old red van in the driveway of the last house on the right. I stopped. I had always wondered where Payton lived and my heart started to beat even faster than it had been, as I thought about the possibility of that being her home.

I crept up the driveway and saw the chipped paint on the back right side of the van and knew for sure that it was the same one Payton drove to school every day. I slowly worked my way toward the front of the van. There was a bike lying on the cement next to a stone walkway, leading to the front door. If I needed any more proof, there was a small wooden sign hanging next to the door that read, "The Carleton's."

When I got closer to the left front bumper I was able to see into a large window which luckily for me didn't have its blinds drawn, like every other house around it. I hoped no neighbors were watching me play "Peeping Tom."

There were people inside walking around and laughing. It was hard to make out details and I couldn't tell if Payton was one of those people. My phone started to ring inside my pocket. I fumbled with the buttons clumsily trying to silence the ringtone.

"Hello," I whispered.

"Mom just got home. Where are you?" Lynn asked. "Why are you whispering?"

"Lynn, I've got to go. I'll be home soon."

"Wait," she quickly said before I could hang up, "the hospital called. Grandpa is finally stable enough to come home."

"Really!" I said, forgetting that I needed to keep my voice low. "That's great," I said more quietly. "I'll be home in a few."

As soon as I hung up, the front door opened. I dove behind the big black garbage can which was next to the garage door and about four feet from the front of the van.

I pressed myself in between the garage and the trash can, praying nobody had noticed me. I just kept imagining someone finding me and seeing how pathetic I probably looked. Sweat was rolling down the bridge of my nose and dripping off its tip onto my knees, which were tucked up to my chest. It was a toss-up between me being so nervous I couldn't control my own sweat glands or because I had just jogged several miles.

It didn't take long before I heard Payton's melodic voice say, "Well, thank you so much for coming. I had a lot of fun."

I prayed even harder that she wouldn't find me.

"I had a great time too. I wouldn't have wanted to spend my evening with any other person."

I froze. She was talking to a guy. Payton started to giggle, which to me sounded unnatural and forced. I didn't dare move, but I wanted to look so badly, I needed to see who she was talking to.

"I will see you at school tomorrow," I heard Payton say. Then I saw the hem of a light blue skirt. They were walking toward the van. I shoved my back into the garage but was still just as visible.

"I can't wait! Save a seat for me at lunch?" I could make out the dark arm of the guy she was with and had a sickening feeling that I knew exactly who he was. When he bent down and picked up the bike that was nearly three feet from me, I could finally see his face. My hunch had been spot on. He was the same kid Payton had been with the day I had followed her out into the school's courtyard.

"Sure," Payton said. I could see both of them clearly. I felt extremely uncomfortable, smashed up against a smelly trash can watching the girl I love flirt with someone else.

I thought I would scream when it looked like the kid was going to make a move and try to kiss Payton. I didn't know what to do. I didn't want to watch that, it was the last thing I wanted to see. It wasn't until then that I realized how Payton must have felt watching Kim and me. Except I am pretty sure I liked her more than she did me.

At the last second, Payton turned her face, offering only her cheek and then gave him a hug. "Be safe," she said.

He looked dejected, only for a second, then hopped onto his bike and said happily, "I always am." She waved to him and watched until he had turned onto the busier street next to her house and was out of view before turning onto the stone walkway.

It wasn't until she had walked out of my view before I could relax. I felt like I had been holding my breath. I was relieved I hadn't been discovered, but felt almost sad that she had left. I wanted to watch her more. I just wanted to be around her. I wanted to take her to prom.

I don't know how that thought had entered my mind. I figured it was because of Lynn. She had gotten me thinking about it and now I had a new resolve. I didn't want her going with anybody else. I decided right then, while hiding from Payton, that if I couldn't go with her to prom I didn't want to go at all. I didn't care about going to the dance, I cared about the person I would hopefully be taking to the dance. I still hadn't forgotten her hatred for me, but I felt that if I didn't try, I would always wonder.

She was walking farther away from me and the words were ready to burst from inside me, before I knew what was happening I yelled, "Payton!"

Sixteen

I was on fire and there was no mistaking that the man sitting in the stands with the red hat was a scout, and everybody knew it. The things he was writing on that yellow notepad he was carrying could easily make or break me. Luckily things seemed to be working out for me perfectly.

We were approaching the end of a no-error game. My team was making me look good, even if it wasn't deliberately. Everybody wanted the chance at getting noticed, so even if some of them hated me, they were willing to cooperate.

I guess the same went for me. One specific highlight of the game was when I barely snagged a fast grounder, turned and threw a rocket to second base. I cringed as soon as I released the ball. I knew I had thrown it too hard. The excitement of the moment had overcome me. B.J. caught the ball effortlessly, tagged the runner and then threw a bullet, faster than I had, to first base. Gus completed the double play.

"Nice catch," I said, nodding to B.J. It felt wrong not acknowledging it.

He looked at me stunned for a second and then a smile crept across his face, "Nice throw," he said.

By the end of the game I had struck out twenty one batters and B.J. had hit three home runs. So it wasn't a surprise when Coach Kline informed us that the scout expressed interest in the two of us.

"You're the one he actually came here for. Congratulations on a great win," B.J. said as soon as Coach had walked away. I gathered my bat bag and glove and walked closer to the bleachers. I thought I had seen Payton in the stands, but maybe it was just hopeful thinking. B.J. followed me.

"Uh, well you deserve to be considered also. You gave us a lot of runs." I had never had a civil conversation with B.J. since we had met. Things still felt forced on my end, but it wasn't as bad as I thought it would be. He played phenomenally that day and he had also impressed me at practice a few days ago when he turned Derek down. I wondered if I had been too hard on him, or maybe I was just in a good mood.

"Thank you," he said.

I stood near the front of the bleachers still trying to find Payton. B.J. stood a few feet away from me. People were coming from everywhere, shaking our hands and congratulating us on the win.

"Boo," Lynn said as she popped out from behind me. "Did I scare you?"

"Oh please, I don't scare easily," I said. "Were you here for the whole game?"

"Yes! And you were awesome. I wanted to make a sign saying 'That's my Brother'," she said with a cheesy grin, which instantly faded the second she noticed B.J. who came to stand next to me.

I didn't want him by us, for Lynn's sake. I also realized that I was the sole cause for the tension between the two of them. Lynn's face was red and I wasn't sure if it was from embarrassment or anger, or maybe it was both.

"Can we talk?" B.J. asked.

I looked down at Lynn, to see her reaction. She was looking at me. "You can do whatever you want," I said to Lynn, "I can give you some privacy, or I can stay right here."

"Actually, I would like for the three of us to talk," B.J. added quickly. He looked nervous. Lynn seemed to relax.

"Okay," I said cautiously.

Joel came over to commend both B.J. and me on a job well done. As soon as he was out of earshot B.J. jumped right in, "I don't have any friends," he said.

I was stunned. I didn't expect that to be what he wanted to talk about, and I think Lynn was just as shocked.

We both looked at each other in confusion and then Lynn let out a little giggle, "Join the party," she said. "Right, Jared?"

B.J. looked at me, innocently. I didn't want to admit that I too had nobody. It would make Derek's statement at practice the other day, that much more looming. I cleared my throat and looked away from both of them. I was looking for an escape.

"What I mean is, *I* understand," Lynn said, pointing to herself. I knew that Lynn had added that last statement for my benefit only, but it kept me from leaving.

"I want to be friends with you two," he said. "And Lynn I need to apologize to you. I am sorry if I treated you wrong in any way and if I made you think that I ...," B.J. started to ramble.

"No, please stop," Lynn begged. "It was me; you didn't do anything." Her face was even redder.

"Well I'm sorry for what happened," he said and then looked at me. "We have had a rough start. I never wanted it to be this way."

I was confused. "How did you want it to be?" I asked, realizing that I had a million questions in my head that I had wanted answers to.

"I thought we would be friends right away. I really didn't think it would be so hard."

"You interjected yourself into every part of my life. I didn't know you. I still don't know you," I said feeling a little worked up. The same emotions I had felt about the situation not that long ago came rushing back.

"I know," B.J. hung his head, "I was overbearing."

"It was creepy!"

"I really didn't want to come across that way."

"One thing still bothers me," I said. B.J. looked up. "What was your intention with Lynn? Was it to get to me?"

B.J. looked at Lynn and then back at me. "You guys act like I had some ulterior motive. I really am being honest when I say that I wanted to be *both* of your friends. That was my intention with Lynn."

Lynn stepped forward. "I'm sorry I've been ignoring you. It wasn't because of what you think. Jared really thought you were using me."

I was still skeptical. It just wasn't normal to have another guy close to your age, whom you barely know, care so much about being a part of your life. "It just seems too weird to me. Why do you care so much?" I said voicing my concerns.

"I really just enjoy your company and to be honest, your family. I really like your family."

I laughed loudly. "We have the most dysfunctional family I know, if you can even call it that."

Lynn scowled at me. "No we don't. Our family's just fine," she said, her voice quivering.

"I have been away from my family for a while. I live with some members of my extended family, as you already know, but it just isn't the same," B.J. said softly.

Lynn smiled warmly at him and said, "We can adopt you into our family."

Both Lynn and B.J. looked at me.

I shrugged, "I still don't know why you would want to. However, I guess we can hang out sometimes. But the weird stuff has got to stop."

"You got it, no more weird stuff," he said smiling.

I noticed Payton in the distance. She was walking to the parking lot. "Payton!" I yelled loudly. Both B.J. and Lynn jumped, apparently startled by my outburst. I thought I could see Payton stop and look over in my direction. "Lynn, do you have a ride home?" I quickly asked without taking my eyes off of Payton.

"Well, I was going to call mom," Lynn started to say.

"Great!" I said, "B.J., I'll catch you later." I ran off before either one of them could say anything else to me.

Payton saw me, but kept walking to her van. I had to speed up to catch her. The whole time I was freaking out. I didn't know what I was going to say. I just knew that I needed to say something. I couldn't choke like I had the night before. Pure instinct had made me call after her out in front of her house, and panic had instantly settled in the second she had turned around.

"Yes? Who's there?" she had asked. My throat had closed off and I pressed myself farther against that trash can and ducked my head in between my knees, hoping she wouldn't hear my sporadic breathing. After a second I could hear her run inside and lock her door.

As I approached Payton, I called her name several times. She finally stopped and turned. I still didn't know what I was going to say, but knew I needed to say something; mainly because I had nowhere to hide this time.

"What do you need, Jared?" she asked.

"Where are you leaving from? I mean, uh, did you see the game?" I knew that I had a bad habit of implying she was solely at that location to see me. She quickly put me in my place.

"No!" she said sarcastically. "I was in the library, studying." Payton held up the three books she was holding and pointed in the direction of the school. "You know Jared, the world doesn't revolve around you ... *my* world doesn't revolve around you," she said slowly, emphasizing every word.

I was tongue-tied. There was no question that this wasn't the right time at all to hint around about prom. But I did want to plead my case. "I am not drinking anymore and I'm not hanging around with the same people that I used to," I said hoping to exonerate myself.

"Was that your choice?"

It *was* my choice.

"Payton," I said, desperately wanting her to believe me. "I am telling you that I am without a doubt, done with it all ... everything, everyone! I am surer of this than of anything I have ever been in my entire life." I was now pacing back and forth in front of her. "I am in the action stage. I have changed my behavior and removed myself from the environment I had been in."

I felt so much emotion. I was no longer trying to convince her. She was just a witness to my monologue. It was then that I realized that I was actively engaged in my own change and that it was happening.

"I am not doing this for you. I am doing it for myself," I said, trying to keep control of my voice, as my emotions overcame me.

She stared at me for a long time. I couldn't hold her gaze. I focused on the black asphalt instead. Finally she grabbed my shoulder so she could make eye contact. A smile crept across her face as she said, "That's what I have been waiting to hear."

Then I watched her walk away, like I always did. Before getting into her van she turned and yelled, "By the way, you played great tonight!"

Seventeen

After the baseball game, and my outburst in the parking lot, I had a glimmer of hope for Payton and me. I didn't feel dread as I walked into psychology class that next morning. I wanted to talk to her more. Impress her more.

I was too late.

From my desk I could see her outside the classroom door. She was holding a large bouquet of flowers and a stuffed animal bear. As she walked inside, her face instantly changed shades. She quickly walked to her desk and shoved the flowers and bear underneath her seat. Everybody was looking at her, including me.

Kim looked from me back to Payton, no doubt trying to decide if I had given them to her. "Did you get asked to prom?" I said. I could see Kim smile out of the corner of my eye.

"Yes," Payton answered, keeping her head low. It seemed like she didn't like the attention she was receiving. "Someone from one of my classes asked me."

"Was it that guy I have seen you with lately?"

"Yes," she answered cautiously, her eyes narrowed. She probably thought I had been spying on her, which was correct. But it had only happened by accident.

"So what's your *friend's* name?" I asked.

"Mitch," she said, "and he's more than just a friend."

"Oh," I said. Those words stung. I faced forward, just to turn back around a second later. "So are you together, like, in a relationship."

Her eyes darted to some of the people sitting around us. "I just don't want to talk about this with you. It's none of your business."

"Ouch!" I heard Derek say, as I turned around. Mrs. Flint had put my project folder on my desk.

"Those of you, who have received your folders today, have a message from your partner. I am anticipating that the others will come tomorrow," Mrs. Flint said cheerfully. "So please take a few minutes to read and respond back, before we move on with today's topic of discussion."

"You crashed and burned," Derek said loudly.

"Mr. Dixon," Mrs. Flint said sternly, "just because you don't have your folder today, I expect you to respect those around you who do."

"Sorry, I will zip it," he said. Once Mrs. Flint sat back at her desk, Derek crouched behind me and whispered into my ear, "You just don't have much to offer, buddy. But I have something that will cheer you up." I knew that Payton could hear him also.

"Kim," Derek said. She looked at me awkwardly for a second and then focused her attention on Derek who was still crouched next to me.

"Yes," she laughed. "What are you doing?"

"Just listen," he said. "You are too hot to be rejected and thrown out. And you are much too hot to not have a date to prom, so what do you say?" Derek held both of his arms out.

Kim didn't look at me again. "Sure ... I mean, yes! I would love to," she said clapping her hands excitedly.

Before sitting down, Derek leaned closer to me and said, "You better hurry before the pickings get slim. You don't want to end up with an ugly freshman."

I needed to get out of that class. I needed to cool down. "Mrs. Flint," I said raising my hand, "can I turn this in to you tomorrow."

"Certainly, take as much time as you need," she was saying as I stood, grabbed my backpack and folder and left. I didn't wait around to see her reaction.

Once I was in my car I screamed and punched my steering wheel a few times. I needed to release some aggression, but it still didn't make me feel better. I kept telling myself that Payton didn't matter and that her love shouldn't be the sole factor in my happiness.

I pulled the paper out of my envelope. The words, "I don't know for sure," from what I had written previously were circled and below it my partner had written, "If you don't know where you are going, how do you know if you get there?"

My partner was right.

I grabbed a pen from my bag and started writing. I filled up the entire first page and flipped it over. After ten minutes I needed to grab another piece of paper from my notebook.

Thoughts and goals just kept flooding my mind. I was jumping head first into this project and there was no turning back. I needed to be completely honest with myself and my partner because I wanted this to work. The grade didn't matter. I needed this to work to help save my life.

I wrote about how I had changed my friends and partying lifestyle. As I wrote, I was convinced that many regrets were saved because of that change. I was trying to be a good person. I mentioned that I was open to even considering a friendship with someone I had hated just a few days ago.

The last thing I wrote about was my family. I knew I could strengthen my relationship with my sister and mom, I decided to make a conscious effort to improve and change our relationship for the better.

"My dad's a different story," was the last thing I had written. "I'm just not willing to go there yet."

I shoved the papers into the envelope and threw it in the backseat of my car. I reclined the driver's side chair and closed my eyes. The warm sun was beating down on my face and I fell asleep.

I remember dreaming about having a different life. I had a brother in my dream. My dad wasn't a jerk. I wasn't a jerk to my dad. Things seemed happier. I used to have dreams like that all the time, but hadn't for a while. I was dreaming about our vacation to the Bahamas. I remember we had a pretty good time as a family. Everyone was getting along, but something was missing. *Someone* was missing.

I dreamt that Bryce was there with us. "Jared!" I heard both Lynn and Bryce calling for me. I was lounging in the sun on a beach towel and they were both swimming in the ocean. "Jared!" I heard their muffled voices call again. Then I heard a strange tapping noise. It got louder.

I opened my eyes and paradise faded away. I couldn't see because the sun was so bright. "Jared, let us in," Lynn said. I unlocked the passenger side door. Lynn unlocked the back side door for B.J.

"How long have you been here?" Lynn looked concerned.

"Is it lunch?" I asked.

Lynn raised her eyebrows and held up two brown paper sacks. I had slept through three of my classes. "This one's for you." Lynn handed one of the sacks to me. "I'm sorry I didn't pack you one B.J. I didn't know if you would be eating with us today."

"That's fine, I have something," he said holding up a sandwich. "Is it okay that I eat with you guys from now on?" he asked.

I looked at him and shrugged. "We just eat here in my car," I said slowly. I still felt groggy. "I don't know why you would want to, but it's fine if you do."

"Thanks," he said.

"Sure."

After a few minutes B.J. asked, "Is this yours? He was holding the manila envelope and some of my papers were spilling out of the top.

"Yes," I said grabbing them out of his hand. He was one of the last people I wanted reading what I had written, it was too personal.

"Grandpa's coming home tonight," Lynn said excitedly to B.J. "You should come over, Mom would love it."

"Okay, I will see if I can. How is he doing? Is he responding to the medicine?" B.J. asked.

Lynn's face fell slightly. "No. Not yet. But mom arranged with hospice to have him come home. A hospice nurse is assigned to Grandpa to help my mom out."

"I see," B.J. said.

"He'll get back to normal. He's going to be fine," Lynn said.

"Do you know what hospice is?" I asked Lynn.

"No."

I looked at B.J. He bit his bottom lip and reached over the seat in front of him to rub Lynn's shoulder as I told her that the hospice nurse's job is to make the patient as comfortable as they can while they die.

"But I thought him coming home meant he was getting better," she cried. I shook my head and then cradled hers against my chest after she had collapsed into me.

Eighteen

Lynn seemed better. She still took the news hard and spent hours after school crying with my mom in her room. Mom was busy getting everything ready for Grandpa. She had moved all of my Grandpa's belongings and furniture into the extra bedroom upstairs. It was smaller than the space he used to have in the basement but made it easier to care for him now. I sat on our front porch steps, at my mom's suggestion, waiting for him and his nurse to show up. I tossed my baseball into the air and let it fall into my glove. I needed to keep my hands busy.

I saw B.J. a few houses away. "You walked here? Where do you live?" I asked when he was close enough.

"Not too far away."

B.J. was holding a rectangular wooden box that had a green bow on top. The wood looked polished and smooth. We both stood quietly. "I'll go get Lynn and my mom," I said. Even with everything that had happened recently, I didn't feel completely comfortable around him.

I opened the front door and yelled, "Mom ... Lynn, B.J.'s here!"

Lynn came to the door first and thanked B.J. for coming. "Come on in B.J.," my mom said as she walked into the foyer. "It's been a while since I've seen you. You need to be visiting us more often."

B.J. looked from Lynn to me and then said, "I will." He then handed the box to my mom. "This is from my Grandma. She wanted your dad to have it as a coming home gift," B.J. said.

"Oh," my mom said taking the gift from B.J. She opened the lid, revealing a small music box. "That's sweet of her." My mom turned a key that was on the top of a small metal rectangle inside of the box. Music filled the room.

"It's the song 'Memory'," B.J. said.

"I know!" My mom smiled. "My dad loves the musical 'Cats'. He and my mom used to dance around the house to it."

"I guess she made a good choice then," said B.J.

My mom carefully closed the lid, and the tinkling sound stopped. "Please, thank your Grandmother for me. We should have her over. I would love to meet her."

"Maybe someday," B.J. said.

"Okay," my mom said slowly. She squinted at him and then smiled. "I will keep pestering you until I get to meet someone. And you should know that any member of your family is a member of ours."

"I'm sure they'll feel that way, too."

"Grandpa's here!" Lynn said loudly, pointing out the door to the large white van parking next to the curb.

"Would you mind putting this on the dresser next to your Grandpa's bed?" My mom handed me the music box and then ran out to meet the nurse.

B.J., Lynn, and I stood alongside an empty wall in the room as they wheeled Grandpa in. He was sitting upright in his wheel chair, but was clearly not coherent.

"Is he okay? Is he awake?" Lynn cried.

My mom and the nurse lifted my Grandpa from his chair to the bed. "Kids, this is Nancy. She is going to be helping me for a while."

Nancy smiled and shook each of our hands. She was a middle aged, plump woman with a friendly face. She was wearing a blue smock with smiley faces all over it. "Your Grandpa is doing just fine," she said to Lynn. "However, the type of cancer he has is spreading very quickly so he is on a lot of pain medications to keep him comfortable."

"Is that why he looks so sleepy?"

"Yes." Nancy smiled. "He will probably be sleepy every day." I knew that was a nice way of saying that we would probably never see him awake again.

The nurse then worked on getting his IV in and making sure he was comfortable. Then she left with my mom to go finish filling out some paperwork. Lynn immediately went to my Grandpa and gave him a big hug, "I'm so glad you're back. I love you, so much," she whispered.

I grabbed his hand and squeezed it a few times, and then said to Lynn, "We should probably let him get some sleep." As Lynn and I were leaving the room, I tensed as I watched B.J. walk to the side of his bed. The feelings I felt that evening in that hospital room were still raw, and I worried how I would react if things repeated themselves.

"Hold on a little longer," B.J. said and then gently lifted the lid to the music box that I had put on the dresser. Hearing that familiar melody was comforting, and I was grateful for B.J. in that moment because, I can't be sure but, it seemed like my Grandpa relaxed even more. B.J. and Lynn left the room and just before I shut the door, I swear I saw my Grandpa smile.

ꕥ

Once the nurse had left for the evening, my mom insisted that B.J. stay for dinner. We ordered pizza and as soon as we had finished eating, B.J. pointed to the glove I had next to me and asked, "Could we go throw the ball around?"

"Sure, I guess."

I stood in the driveway so that we could have enough space. We threw the ball back and forth to each other without saying anything. I felt a little awkward, but enjoyed hearing the audible "smack" every time the ball hit our gloves.

"It's nice playing catch without having you try to take my head off," B.J. said after a while. He smiled sheepishly as I caught the ball and held it.

I needed to loosen up. I finally smiled and then threw the ball back. "I'm sorry about that," I said.

"It actually helped my eye-hand coordination," he said.

"Well, I am glad to be of some assistance."

"Too bad you don't have some kind of drill to improve Derek's eye-foot coordination," B.J. said with a straight face.

I couldn't tell if he was serious or joking. I wanted to laugh but held it in. I worried that I would end up snorting or something. I finally managed to ask, "Did you happen to see the hole before

Derek stepped into it?" I had thought I saw B.J. slowly pushing Derek toward it while we had been jogging.

"I swear," B.J. shook his head and held up his pointer and middle fingers, "scouts honor."

"I wasn't sure at the time," I said. "It worked out perfectly though. If I'm being honest, I have to say ... I did see it and was focused on it the entire time."

B.J. smirked. "Well, if I'm being honest, I have to say ... I never was a boy scout."

I stared at B.J. as his words slowly sank in, and when they did, I laughed out loud. I laughed harder than I had in a long time. I kept picturing Derek's face just before it smashed into the ground. I was quickly losing control. "I didn't realize you were so funny," I said trying to gain some composure. "I appreciate people who have a sense of humor."

B.J. smiled.

I threw the ball to him and once again started to laugh. "We really need to talk about something else, before I bust a gut."

B.J. threw the ball back and I caught it just as my dad was pulling into the driveway. I stepped into the grass so he could park in the garage and threw the ball back. He didn't close the garage and instead of going into the house he came out into the yard.

"Hello, Mr. Anderson," B.J. said politely.

"Hello. Lynn's friend," my dad said slowly.

"It's B.J.," I said, without looking at him.

"Right," my dad said. "I'm sorry."

"No problem," B.J. said. "Would you like to join us?" He held up the baseball.

I looked at my dad. I hadn't played catch with him since I was at least twelve years old. I was shocked to see that he looked like he was considering it. He looked back and forth at the two of us, and I wondered if that was the reason he chose to walk past us rather than go inside through the garage, like he always did.

My dad looked at me for a moment. I imagined that my face was completely expressionless. "I better get inside. I have some paper work I need to file," my dad said as he tapped his briefcase with his finger. He looked at me a second longer, nodded to B.J. and then walked inside.

B.J. threw the ball back to me. "If I weren't here, would he have played?" he asked.

"Nope." I threw it back. "He may have if I weren't, though." B.J. turned the ball in his hand, and I could tell he had something on his mind. "Go ahead and ask," I said.

"Ask what?"

"My dad and I have a strained relationship. As if you hadn't noticed," I said. I lifted my glove up and opened and shut it a few times, urging B.J. to throw the ball back.

He didn't. "Why?" he asked instead.

"He'd probably blame it on puberty or hormones. He'd call me rebellious and disrespectful." I started rambling. "I guess I am those things, but I could feel him distancing himself from me. That's when I realized that he wanted a different son. He wanted one who didn't make mistakes all the time."

I sat down on the steps in front of my house and B.J. started to walk toward me. I had never vocalized those types of feelings before, but I couldn't stop. "He's never said this, but I am positive, that if my dad could change the past he would have chosen to have buried a different son ... maybe he would have had better luck with my brother," I said ending my rant.

B.J. stood next to me, but was looking away.

"Sorry man, you probably don't want to hear my family's twisted life story, or maybe you already have. Did Lynn fill you in on what happened?"

"She did, a little ... but I'd kind of like to hear it from you," B.J. said.

He continued to stare away.

I couldn't blame him for feeling uncomfortable. I couldn't believe I was even talking to him about that stuff. It wasn't until I had started talking that I realized how much I needed to. I had never talked about how it felt having a dead brother to anyone. I was a closed person, much like my dad. But also, no one ever asked me about it until today. No one seemed to care to ask how *I* was doing, and ironically enough the person I had wanted completely out of my life less than a week ago, was that "one person" who cared enough to ask.

"I was young, so I don't remember a lot. I was barely over a year old." I picked at the grass next to my foot. B.J.'s head was down and he was turning the baseball over and over in his hands. "All I know is that I had a brother, he died before he ever left the hospital, and his name was ... Bryce." I hadn't said his name out loud since I was young. It felt weird, like I shouldn't be saying it.

B.J. finally looked at me. He was crying. "I'm sorry," he said. I couldn't believe he was so emotional. I felt embarrassed for him. "You mentioned that you *had* a brother, but isn't he still your brother?" B.J. asked.

"I don't believe in that kind of stuff."

"In what stuff?"

"Heaven, angels ... those kinds of things," I answered.

"I do," he said.

Nineteen

My partner was trying my patience. "Make a list of things you could do to develop a better relationship with your dad," was written in my folder. This person wasn't messing around and apparently didn't understand what I meant when I said, "I am not willing to go there yet."

"Change will most often come at its own pace," Mrs. Flint said after she had finished passing folders out. "It can come quickly and in bursts, rather than keep a steady pace. It is actually quite normal for someone to spend years in 'pre-contemplation' and then jump to 'action' in a matter of weeks."

That was my story.

"Unfortunately, while in the beginning of the action stage there is the possibility of a regression, like Ms. Carleton had suggested not that long ago."

I slumped in my chair. Payton had been referring to me that day. I wondered if she still felt the same way.

I grabbed my paper and finished reading what my partner had written, "I think it is great that you have changed so many things already, but if you don't decide to change everything that you have committed to, it will be too easy to go back to your old life."

I kind of wished I hadn't committed to that.

My initial instinct was to stuff the paper back into the envelope blank. I resisted the urge to write, "I don't know what to do," and then I started thinking. If I actually had ideas of things I could do to improve my relationship with my dad, wouldn't I have already done it?

I wasn't so sure I would have. I did know that on that specific day, I wanted more than anything for things to change between the two of us.

"Swallow my pride," was the first thing I wrote.

I felt a tap on my back.

I didn't dare turn around. I was too worried I had imagined it. After a little bit I heard Payton whisper, "Jared, I just wanted to say that I didn't mean to sound so rude yesterday."

I stared down at my paper and couldn't deny the irony of what I had just written. "I hope you have a great time with Mitch," I said almost choking on the last word.

And that was the end of the conversation. I wasn't sure if she thought I was being genuine. I wouldn't have held it against her if she hadn't, because I wasn't sure myself.

"Learn to forgive," was the next thing I wrote.

The bell had already rung and most of the classroom was empty. "Will changing someone's life, change yours as well?" was the last thing I wrote to my partner before handing Mrs. Flint my folder. I was curious if this person were getting anything worthwhile out of this project, or if dealing with my issues were enough of a project.

"Jared." Mrs. Flint stopped me from leaving. "I just wanted to let you know that your work ethic has not gone unnoticed. I appreciate your dedication to this class project." She was smiling broadly.

"Thank you," I said trying to leave. But she wasn't done.

"If only the entire class could embrace their desire to 'change' as much as you have ... I would be ecstatic."

"Yep," I said, inching toward the door.

"Maybe you should talk to that friend of yours, Derek, and help him get his act together," she said.

I had made it out the door and was standing in the hall. "Oh, he's not my friend anymore," I said before waving and telling her I needed to get to my next class.

ꟸ

"Are you going to prom?" I asked B.J., once we were a few feet away from the rest of the baseball team. Everyone was stretching and warming up as we waited for Coach Kline to get there.

"No, are you?"

"I'm thinking about it," I said. I sounded unsure.

"Are you thinking of asking that girl you chased down the other day?" B.J. put a weight at the end of his bat.

"No," I said quickly. "She already has a date." He took a few practice swings. "She'll never be interested in me anyway," I added.

"Never say never," B.J. grunted as he swung the bat.

I looked around. A majority of the team was unloading their gear in the dugout. Derek, Gus, and a few others were walking to the baseball diamond from the locker room.

"No ... I was thinking of taking someone else," I said.

B.J. stopped swinging. "Who?" he asked.

"Well isn't this a surprise," Derek said loudly as soon as he had walked through the chain link gate onto the field. "The two loners have found each other, and it looks like they are friends!"

I turned away from Derek and continued to stretch my arms and legs. B.J. continued practicing his swing. "What's the deal B.J.? I offer you a great opportunity and you turn me down for what ... Jared?" Derek shook his head, and clicked his tongue. "I thought you were smarter than that."

B.J. continued to swing his bat, expressionless. "You would rather spend your time around someone who hated your guts?"

B.J. opened his mouth to say something but I cut him off by saying, "You're right Derek, and doesn't that make you crazy thinking that he would rather be around someone who couldn't stand him than be around someone like you?"

"You piece of ...," Derek started to say just as Coach Kline walked onto the field.

"You have five more minutes to warm up and then line up for batting practice," Coach yelled.

"I'm sorry about what I said. I didn't mean ...," I started to say to B.J.

"Don't worry about it." B.J. waved his hand, interrupting me. "It needed to be said."

We were running laps at the end of practice when B.J. caught up to me. "So who?" he asked.

"What?" I said, even though I knew what he meant.

"Who are you thinking of asking to the dance?"

I suddenly got nervous. I wasn't sure what B.J. would think about it. "Lynn," I finally said. "I was thinking of asking Lynn."

When I finally looked at B.J., he smiled and then said, "I was hoping that was who you were going to say."

"You don't think that's weird?"

"Why would I think that?" He seemed genuinely confused.

"I don't know," I said quickly. "I'm her only brother and I need to protect her and be there for her."

"But you aren't her only brother."

I looked at B.J. and laughed. He stared at me, his brow furrowed.

"You know what I mean. And I already talked to you about this, I don't believe in that stuff," I said.

"I like to think that I will see certain members of my family who aren't with me now," B.J. said. We were quite a few feet apart from the rest of the team. We must have picked up our pace without knowing it. "Does that not give you any kind of comfort?"

"No, it doesn't, much like this conversation," I said sharply.

"I'll back off if you want me to," B.J. said quietly. "Just say the word." When I didn't say anything, he added, "Have you always felt this way?"

I intentionally picked up the pace. I didn't want anyone else on the team overhearing. "When I was young, I thought I would see him again. I used to pretend that he was with me sometimes."

"What changed?" Derek asked.

"I got older and stopped living in a delusional world," I said bitterly. B.J. looked at me like he expected more of an explanation.

I sighed and then said between breaths, "One day when I was six our family went to an arcade. I was having so much fun playing the games that I said to my parents, 'Could we come back here with Bryce one day?' I was just thinking how fun it would have been to play some of the games with him."

I knew B.J. was staring at me, but I refused to look at him. I felt stupid admitting my morbid childish fantasy. "And to make a long story short, my dad lost it. He started yelling at me, telling me that it was time for me to grow up and face the facts," I said. I was grateful that we were running at that moment. It was easier to disguise the strain in my voice. "I never talked about him again."

"Maybe your dad was trying to ...," B.J. started to say.

"Don't make excuses for him," I interrupted forcefully, then softened my voice to say, "Actually I agree with his message, just not the delivery."

"Are you sure you do?" B.J. asked.

"You bet," I said.

We were getting close to the end of our run and B.J. seemed deep in thought, until we passed by a dark spot in the grass. A smile spread across my face as soon as B.J. pointed at it and hollered, "Derek! Watch out for that hole in the grass!"

Twenty

"Wow!" was all I could say. She looked so beautiful. Lynn blushed and looked at her feet.

"You're just saying that," she whispered, "because you're my brother."

"Tonight I'm more than your brother, I'm your date," I said. "And I mean it when I say you look so pretty tonight." Lynn was wearing a long light purple dress, and her hair was curled and pinned up. My mom had sewn a matching headband for her to wear.

"Where are your glasses," I asked, suddenly realizing the biggest difference in her appearance.

"Mom got me some contacts," she said shyly.

"What did I say about wearing contacts," I teased.

"It's only for tonight." Lynn's face beamed.

My mom had handed B.J. her camera, so she could wipe her eyes. "You two look so wonderful," she cried. We stood in the entryway as B.J. took pictures of Lynn pinning the boutonniere to my suit jacket. "Say cheese!" he said.

"All right, that's enough," I said as I tried to grab the camera. B.J. dodged me and managed to take a close up shot of my face.

"Now that's a keeper!" He laughed.

"You guys should start thinking about leaving," my mom said.

"Do you want us to drop you off at your house before we head to the dance?" I said to B.J. as I pulled my keys out of my pocket.

"No, I can walk," B.J. said and then turned to my mom. "I was actually wondering if I could stay a little bit longer. I could help you out, since Nancy is sick and all." My Grandpa's nurse had called yesterday to inform us that she had strep throat and wouldn't be coming to the house until she was completely healthy.

My mom was under strict orders to call and report any changes with Grandpa. The past week or so, his condition had gone drastically downhill. We were just buying time now. Today was when I started to notice it wearing on her.

"You do look tired mom. B.J. could help you out and let you get some rest," I added.

She looked at me and then back at B.J., "I bet you have plenty of things you would rather be doing on a Friday evening than hanging out with some old lady and her sick dad," she said.

"Mrs. Anderson, I would really like to help out tonight. Please let me." B.J. almost sounded as if he was pleading for her to let him stay.

For the past month, ever since he and I became friends, we had started seeing more and more of B.J. At first he would come by a few times a week, but now, it is more like every day. It had actually been kind of nice, and I think everyone else felt the same way. It's like he had become a part of the family.

"You know, you are a very special person," my mom said as she touched B.J.'s arm. "If you want to stay, I'm not stopping you." She smiled.

"Great!" B.J. said. "My family has a lot going on tonight, so I won't be missed."

We all turned when the front door opened. My dad set his briefcase on the sofa and went to stand next to my mom. "I was worried I would miss seeing you guys leave," he said. "My meeting ran late," he said to my mom before kissing her on the forehead. He seemed to be in a good mood.

Lynn gave me a surprised smile before she asked, "How do I look Daddy?"

As my dad looked at her his eyes started to water. He quickly cleared his throat and said, "You don't look like my little girl anymore."

Lynn smiled and ran to him. She hugged him tightly around the waist as he looked up at me. "I expect my daughter to be home no later than twelve o'clock sharp."

"Yes sir," I said.

"You guys are so weird." Lynn looked up at my dad and giggled. My mom pulled Lynn from my dad to take some pictures of her with B.J.

My dad walked closer to me and grabbed my shoulder. "I just want to let you know how impressed I am by your choice to ask Lynn to this dance," he whispered into my ear. "I ...," he started to choke up, "don't give you enough credit for the things you do right, son."

I swallowed my pride. "I wanted to do this ... for her," I said. My dad patted my shoulder one more time.

ꕤ

"I'm so nervous, Jared."

We stood right outside the gym doors. Through the window we could see lights, flowers, and a lot of people. The loud music vibrated the handles on the door.

"Just take a deep breath," I said. I breathed in deeply with her. "And remember, I'm here with you."

I think Lynn was a little overwhelmed. She held onto my arm tightly as we wound our way through people to the tables. "I just want to sit down for a little bit," she had said as soon as we walked in.

"What's up All-Star?" Gus said as I was pouring some juice into a cup for Lynn. I looked back at Lynn. She was sitting at a table waiting for me, when a group of people walked up to her.

"Nothing," I said quickly as I grabbed the cup and left.

"Is everything all right here," I said loudly, shoving my way through the group to Lynn. I saw Lindsey and some other people I didn't know. I did however recognize the boy with the jet black hair. He was one of the guys whom I had attacked for taunting Lynn. The second he saw the look on my face, he took a few steps back.

Lynn stood and grabbed my arm. "This is Adam, and he was just apologizing to me," Lynn said.

"I just wanted to introduce myself to her and let her know that I am really sorry for what happened that day," he stammered.

"You look really pretty, Lynn," Lindsey said.

"Thank you." Lynn looked at her feet.

I continued to stare at the group of people in front of me. I wasn't willing to let my guard down. I caught a few of the guys looking at Lynn. They seemed interested, and I didn't like it. Just then a slow song started to play. I grabbed Lynn and led her out to the dance floor. I walked past them without a word. Lynn waved feebly and said, "I'll see you later," to Lindsey.

"I don't want you becoming friends with those people," I said as soon as we had started dancing.

"I'll be careful," she said. "Besides, next week I'll be back to being the glasses wearing loner with no friends."

"Hey, I take offense to that, and I'm pretty sure B.J. would, too," I said.

"You're right. With friends like you two, who needs more?" She laughed.

"You're a pretty good dancer," I said to Lynn after a while.

She looked at me and smiled and then her face grew serious. Her eyes started to water. "What's the matter?" I asked.

"Jared, thank you so much for bringing me to prom. I am having so much fun," she cried.

"Then you need to be happy," I said, teasing her. "And I'm sorry that I'm not some boy you have a crush on or something."

"No," she said laughing. "You're even better, you're my brother."

Lynn put her head against my chest, and that was when I noticed Payton. She was staring at us. She was dancing with her date, Mitch, whose back was to me. She smiled, and I saw a tear run down her cheek.

Later that night when I was coming out of the restroom, Payton stopped me. "Were you waiting for me?" I asked, looking back at the wall next to the boy's bathroom, where she had been standing.

"Yes," she said laughing.

"That's what I thought." I smiled.

She looked so good, it was hard to focus. And when she walked up close to me, I thought I might pass out. "You are a good person, Jared," she said. "I hate thinking that I've made you feel like you weren't."

I started to speak, but she gently touched my face, stopping me. My heart stopped. "What you did for your sister tonight is ...," she paused, "there are no words for it. It's pure kindness." She started crying. "I just wanted you to know how amazing you are."

A slow song started playing and it echoed through the empty hall. "Dance with me," Payton said.

"Sure." I had never been a good dancer, but didn't care as long as I could hold her.

"That wasn't a question," she said as she wrapped her arms around my neck.

The song didn't last long enough.

"Thank you," she whispered and then kissed me on the cheek before walking back to the gym. I stood there for I don't know how long, reliving what had just happened, and praying for more.

Once I got back to the gym, even from a distance, I could tell something was wrong. Lynn had her phone in her hand and her face was pale. "It's Grandpa," she said.

"Gus told me you were here ... and I just had to see for myself." Derek was blocking the exit. Lynn had been behind me, following me, as I fought my way through the crowd. I grabbed her arm and pulled her next to me.

Lynn was trying to be brave but I could see she was going to lose it soon. "I don't have time for this. Save all your insults for another day. We have a family emergency and need to go, now," I said.

Derek's face changed. "Wow, Lynn, you're so grown up. You look great."

I could tell he was being genuine, at least when it came to Lynn. "Can we go now?" I said sharply.

Kim walked to stand next to Derek. She looked at me and then Lynn. "Is this your sister?" she asked quietly.

"Yes," I said impatiently. "We need to go, now."

Kim didn't take her eyes off of me as I walked past them and out the doors. "Don't get used to this kind of treatment All-Star. It just so happens that I'm in a good mood tonight," Derek yelled as Lynn and I ran to my car.

Twenty-One

I hated funerals. There was just something so final about them. I was suffocating being in that room with all those people. I managed to make my way to the exit after only being stopped a few times as people offered their condolences.

"I'm so sorry about your Grandpa Miller. Just remember that he lived a good full life and is back with his sweetheart now," said an ancient lady, who looked like she already had one foot in the grave.

"I suppose so," I said. "I just need to get some air." I pushed past her to the doors. An afternoon breeze blew in my face helping me relax a little. I loosened my tie after I plopped down on the parking lot curb.

"May I join you?"

I was surprised to see Payton standing a few feet from me. "Sure," I said pointing to the curb, "it's super comfortable."

She joined me and we sat in silence. It was calming having her there. The finality of what had happened was starting to hit me, and I just needed someone by me.

"Uh, how did you know about the funeral?" I asked after I had gained some composure.

"Your friend B.J. told me about it. He said that you would want me here today."

I smiled and said without looking at her, "He was right."

Payton slipped her arm through mine and said, "If there is anything you need to talk about."

"I appreciate you being here," I said.

"I heard that it happened the night of prom." Payton bit the bottom of her lip nervously and then asked, "Did you at least get to see him before he ...?" She didn't finish her sentence.

It was still bittersweet thinking back at that night. It happened a little over a week ago, but it almost felt like a distant memory. At least he wasn't in pain anymore, I kept telling myself.

"Yes, barely," I said.

"That's good."

"B.J. was there helping that night. My mom started to realize that Grandpa didn't have much longer and called Lynn so we could see him one last time." I tried to keep my emotions under control. "I was able to say goodbye," I said as I started to cry. I couldn't hold it in any longer. "He could barely move and he would mumble every now and then. It seemed like he wanted to tell me something ... I just couldn't understand what he was saying. I've stayed up the last few nights wondering what he was trying to tell me, and if it was important."

Payton squeezed my arm.

Lynn had had a difficult time that night. She had hugged him one last time and then needed to leave the room. My mom had gone to check on her when B.J. walked up to my grandpa. He placed the music box next to him and then lifted the lid. "Goodbye," he had said quietly as the music started playing. Then my grandpa relaxed as he took his last breath.

"Do you think that he is gone forever ... like he no longer exists?" I asked after a long pause.

Instead of answering my question Payton asked, "What do you think?"

"I think people choose to believe that, because it makes them feel better to think that someday they will get to see those who have died," I said.

"It makes *me* feel better," she said. "And I actually do believe it."

"So does B.J.," I said quietly. Payton smiled and then squeezed my arm again. It felt so good having her by me and talking to me. "Did you know that I had a brother who died?" I asked, wanting to let her know more about me.

"No, I didn't. I'm so sorry," she gasped.

"It was a long time ago," I said smiling at her. Her concerned face looked so cute. I got serious as a thought crossed my mind, "So you also believe that I will see my brother again?"

Payton looked at me for a long time. "I believe it with all my heart," she finally whispered.

"It'll be interesting to see if you and B.J. are right," I said, trying to look skeptical.

"If there's one thing you should know about me by now, it's that I'm always right." She smiled.

"It'd actually be okay if you were," I said, nudging her playfully. "Payton," I said in a more serious tone. She looked up at me. "I hope you know that there is more to me than what people think at school." I didn't know how to put into words what I wanted her to know. I just wanted her to see the real side of me.

"I knew your potential long before I think *you* ever did," she said. "It is May eighth, we still have a month left before summer break, and you have already changed into the person I knew you could always be."

I had a pretty good idea what she was getting at and laughed when she said, "If I were your partner I would suggest to Mrs. Flint that you deserve extra credit."

"If only I could be so lucky," I said. I couldn't keep my eyes off her. Just talking to her had made me feel better. She had given me hope. "I want to thank you for the notes," I said. I got embarrassed and looked at the ground, "Especially the ones that were blunt and to the point. I needed to hear it."

"You're welcome," she said quietly. I still wondered what it was that made her care so much about me to even bother. Then I thought about my mom, and when she had read the notes under my mattress. "This is someone who see's in you, exactly what I do," she had said.

People were still arriving.

"Jared, I'm sorry, but I won't be able to stay long. I need to babysit for my parents for a couple of hours," Payton said apologetically as she watched the people go into the building.

I didn't want her to leave. I wanted to keep talking in hopes that things would start to get back to normal between the two of us. "Come meet my mom first," I said quickly, "if that's okay?"

"Sure." She stood and straightened out her dress.

I grabbed her hand and led her to my family. It was the first time we ever held hands. It felt natural. "Mom, I want you to meet Payton Carleton; we go to school together," I said, as soon as I had found her. My mom smiled and as she shook Payton's hand, I whispered, "The note girl." Her smile brightened as she pulled Payton aside and started asking her questions about herself and her family.

"Son, can we talk?" My dad had come up behind me. I nodded and he pointed to a sofa close to where we were standing.

We sat down. "I'm sorry about Grandpa," he said. He scratched his head and avoided eye contact. "I don't do well at funerals." He cleared his throat. "Are uh ... you okay?" He asked uncomfortably.

"I'm fine," I lied.

"Well, I'm here if you want to talk." I knew he was being sincere but I also knew that he was probably praying I wouldn't need to talk, especially about my feelings.

"All right ... thanks Dad."

My mom was wiping her eyes with a tissue and then gave Payton a hug. They must have started talking about Grandpa. A few feet from them were B.J. and Lynn. They were next to the casket and seemed like they were deep in discussion. B.J. rubbed Lynn's back as she started to cry. We watched them for a while and then my dad cleared his throat, "He's a good friend. I like him." He nodded in B.J.'s direction.

"Yes, he's growing on me," I said.

I could tell my dad had more he wanted to say. "So ...," I finally said, seeing if that would move things along. It looked like my mom and Payton were saying their goodbyes and I wanted to ask her one more thing before she left.

My dad looked at me and I could see determination in his eyes. "I have known for a long time that life is short," he finally said. I looked down at my hands. "And instead of making the most of the time I have had with my family I have pushed everyone away. I have pushed you away."

I felt a knot in my chest.

"I figured that if you don't get too attached, it won't hurt so badly when it is taken from you," he continued to say, "and you guys have paid the price for my actions ... and I apologize for that."

My dad looked beaten down. I don't think he had ever voiced his feelings so frankly before in his life. "Okay," was all I could say, and I knew that that was all he needed to hear. Without speaking another word, he patted my knee, stood, and left the room.

I didn't move. I let everything sink in. I realized that within the last five minutes my relationship with my dad had changed. It was slightly stronger. I felt a weight lift from my shoulders.

"You *will* see him again!"

I jumped. B.J. was standing right next to me. "I didn't see you coming," I said quickly. I had been deep in thought. I looked up at him, "You mean my Grandpa, right?"

"Sure," he replied.

"And other people," I said, knowing what he would say.

"I know it, Lynn knows it ... your mom knows it," he said quietly.

I looked over at Lynn. She was leaning over the casket peering in at Grandpa, wiping her eyes feverishly, but she had a smile on her face.

"Why?" I asked, "There's no proof."

"You can feel it."

I started to shake my head when B.J. pointed to my chest. As soon as his finger touched my shirt I instantly felt warm. It was like my body had been covered in frost bite and someone had just placed a warm blanket over me. My fingertips tingled. I felt shockwaves pulsing through my body, but this time I didn't feel uncomfortable, it felt comforting.

"What is going on?" I asked breathlessly.

B.J. looked at me with a puzzled expression. He then tried to suppress a smile as he said, "I don't know ... maybe you're feeling it." His hand dropped and the warmth stayed for a few seconds more, and then slowly went away. "You're the only one who can convince yourself," he said before walking back to Lynn.

I didn't want that feeling to leave. For those few seconds everything happening in my life seemed better.

"I'm going to go." Payton touched my hand.

"Okay," I said, trying to hide my face. I wasn't sure if I was visibly crying because inside I was sobbing like a baby.

She waved to Lynn and B.J. and before she had reached the door, and after I gained some composure, I ran to her and asked, "Tonight can we go for a walk together?"

She looked at me funny, and then nodded. "Actually that sounds nice."

"I'll come by around seven."

Payton watched me from the corner of her eye and then started to say, "I live off of ..."

"I know where you live," I interrupted without thinking.

"You do?"

"Uh ... yes," I answered sheepishly.

She shook her head and then finally smiled. "I'll see you at seven."

ꝏ

The day seemed never ending. I walked to Payton's house, because I wanted to have a few minutes to myself. After the graveside service a few family members and friends came over to the house. Lynn and my mom had worked all the night before preparing platters of food. Unlike them, I had gotten enough sleep that night, but I felt so tired. I guess I was just emotionally exhausted.

I found Payton's house easily, and got nervous walking up to her front door. No other person had that effect on me. She answered the door and was still wearing the black skirt she had been wearing at the funeral. I felt underdressed and out of place in my old jeans. But she looked beautiful.

"I'm ready for our walk," she said. "Where are we going?"

"Is it okay if I show you something?"

"Sure," she said excitedly.

I grabbed her hand before I would lose my nerve. I hoped she was okay with it, since I did hold her hand earlier that day. I smiled when she rubbed the inside of my wrist with her thumb. "Where are we going?" she asked after we had been walking for a couple of minutes.

"Almost there," I said. I wasn't sure what she would think about where I was taking her.

We crossed the main street to the Boulder City Cemetery. "Are we going inside," Payton asked. Surprisingly she didn't sound apprehensive at all.

"I wanted to, if that's okay with you?"

"It's okay with me," she said.

We walked on the pathway that led to the spot where my brother was buried. Once we got close I directed her off the path and onto the grass where we walked a few feet.

"Wow, that pine tree has gotten big," I said, as I walked by the dark giant.

"How long has it been since you have been here?" Payton asked in a whisper. I thought it was cute that she felt the need to be quiet.

"It's been a while." I felt ashamed. We walked a few steps more when I pointed to a gray stone sticking out of the ground, "That's it."

Payton bent down and lightly touched the engraving of a teddy bear on the left side of the stone. "It's beautiful," she said and then crouched closer. "Bryce James Anderson, June fourteenth, nineteen ninety seven," she read aloud.

"It's been almost sixteen years," I said.

Payton stood up and walked over to me. "Do you do anything special on June fourteenth?" she asked.

"Not really. We used to all come here as a family and bring flowers. When I was young I would always leave one of my toys behind. I guess I thought one day he would be able to play with them." I laughed at myself. "For the past few years my mom has gone by herself."

"Why don't the rest of you go anymore? Why doesn't your father?"

"I was thinking about what you said earlier today, that you believed with all your heart that I would see Bryce again one day." My voice started shaking. "I think that my mom believes that she will see her son again. So coming here isn't as painful for her as it is for my dad. It's like therapy to her."

"Maybe being here would be good therapy for all of you," she said.

I nodded. I had been thinking that same thing. If just believing that I would see Bryce again could give me a fragment of comfort like I had felt earlier that day, I would never stop believing. Payton instinctively rubbed the sides of her arms when the breeze started to pick up.

"I should get you back home, it's getting late," I said. "I hope I didn't ruin our first date by taking you to a cemetery at night," I said.

"So this is a date?"

My body went numb. "Uh ... I thought so, unless you don't think it is," I stammered.

She laughed and then poked me in the chest. "I think it is whatever you think it is," she teased.

"I wouldn't say that if I were you," I said. "Because I think I like you way more than you realize."

She blushed.

"Before we go, I need to ask you something," I said. She looked up at me and her face grew serious as I tried to find the courage to speak. "I want this to be the first of many dates and I want to have a relationship with you."

Payton's smile returned.

"And if that is something you want, too, then Mitch has to go," I blurted out.

"Oh really," she said. She let go of my hand to place her hands on her hips.

"Yes," I said less confidently. "I'm far from perfect and I don't know him that well, but there is no way he cares about you more than I do."

Her surprised eyes looked at me and then she wrapped her arms around my waist and laid her head on my chest. I cradled her and gently kissed the top of her head. I had dreamed of being able to hold her like that, but never thought that I ever would.

"There never was anything between Mitch and me." She looked up at me. Her beautiful blue eyes held me captive.

"Nothing?"

"I tried to see if there was something," she said quietly. "But I just can't get away from you Jared." I couldn't believe what I was hearing. "You feel right ... if that makes any sense."

She laid her head back on my chest. I slowly stroked her hair and said, "I know what you're saying." I thought I was going to burst. I could have stood there with her for eternity. "I don't want to ever disappoint you again," I whispered. "You're too important to me."

She straightened and placed her arms behind my head. She looked me in the eyes as she said, "And you are important enough to me that if you do ... I won't abandon you again. Just realize that you have to feel that you're important enough not to disappoint yourself."

I couldn't look away. I didn't dare. My heart was pounding so hard I swear she could hear it. "I'm about to do something ... that I'm really nervous about," I said.

She smiled and held my gaze, and that was when I kissed her.

Twenty-Two

Summer vacation had finally come. The last month of school had gone by too quickly. It's ironic that instead of welcoming summer, I actually had wished time would slow down. Things with Payton and I couldn't have been going any better. I saw something special with her.

Baseball was over now. I hated to see the season end because I love the game so much. Luckily, I have some great memories from the last few games. It was nice seeing Payton in the stands cheering me on. But it was even nicer having my parents and Lynn there to watch B.J. and me. My dad had even cancelled meetings so he could make it to some of my games and I swear that I played better when he was there.

"I am expecting great things from you boys next year," Coach Kline had yelled to B.J. and me, while we were talking to my family after our last game.

"You bet," I yelled back.

"And B.J., keep your swing strong on the off season," he said, "I get two more years with you before you graduate." Coach Kline was in a good mood. We had managed to tie for first place in our region, and Coach was ecstatic. He expected an even better record for the next year.

"See you Coach," B.J. said. He had been more quiet than usual. "Thank you for everything you have done."

"No problem," Coach said.

My dad watched Coach Kline leave and then said, "I'm looking forward to seeing you boys play next year. And uh ... I will try to make it to more games."

"Cool," I said. I actually was excited to show my dad more of my talent.

B.J. looked distracted.

"Honey ... is everything all right?" my mom asked him.

"Oh, yes, I'm fine," B.J. said quickly. "I just had such a great time playing baseball and going to school and spending time with you guys."

"Well, look at it this way, you get a break from school and baseball to relax and sleep in," my mom said as she laughed. "The only thing you won't get a break from is us."

"I don't want one," B.J. said quietly.

"Well, should we all get back home," my dad said. "Your mom and I thought we would have a family barbeque tonight. You can come too B.J., if you want?" My dad was starting to get over his awkwardness around B.J.

"Of course, I'm starving," he said.

We were almost to the parking lot when I noticed Payton standing by my car. "B.J., is it okay if you ride with my parents?" I asked. I subtly nodded in Payton's direction.

B.J.'s eyes widened and then he said, "Sure," before he winked at me.

"I'll meet you guys at the house," I said as they drove away.

Payton walked up to me and smiled. "I saw some of your game. I missed the first few innings but I am pretty sure you played amazingly."

She still knew how to make me blush. I hated it, but loved it at the same time. She handed me a large manila folder she had been holding.

"Is this my psych project?"

"Yes, that is why I was late getting to your game."

I opened up the tab and pulled out a thick stack of papers. "Mrs. Flint stopped me in the hall and wanted me to give that to you."

"Why?" I asked.

"She just said that she felt you may want them," Payton said shrugging her shoulders.

"I threw this away two days ago," I said more to myself than to Payton.

Mrs. Flint had handed back our projects at the beginning of the week. It was our last grade before the end of the year. I had only glanced to see that I had gotten the same grade I had given my partner and then threw it in the trash can outside of the class.

"She must had seen it and pulled it out," Payton said.

"I guess so," I mumbled as I flipped through the papers.

"I need to go; my family is waiting for me," Payton said. "We are all going out to dinner." She kissed me on the cheek.

"Isn't that just adorable." I turned and saw Derek holding his bat bag.

"Bye," Payton said as she ran to her car. She kept her eye on Derek as she unlocked her van.

"Can I call you tonight," I called to her.

Payton smiled and then said, "You'd better!"

"No really, I mean it, absolutely adorable," Derek said.

"What do you want?"

Derek's face became serious and he fiddled with the strap on his bag. "I just wanted to let you know that even though you are a complete sell out now, you still know how to play ball like an All-Star," he finally said.

"Oh ... really!?" I said boastfully.

"If anyone asks I will deny it," Derek said pointing to me.

I grinned as big as I could. He shook his head and then turned to leave, but before he turned I saw a smile spread across his face.

Instead of getting into my car, I leaned against it as I finished flipping through the papers I was holding. I re-read some of the things I had written about my dad. I had been so bitter and some of the things made me cringe. But then my tone started to change. I started listing anything positive that would happen between my dad and me, even the tiniest of things. Toward the end of the stack of papers I had written, "One day my dad said that he noticed I was almost out of toothpaste and then he threw me a new tube that he had taken out of his bag. It made me feel like there is hope for us."

"That's because there is," my partner had written.

As the weeks had progressed my suggestions had started getting lengthier as I became more involved in my partner's efforts for "change," even if it was an unusual goal. "If my life is changed while I try to change someone else's then it will make everything I am doing worthwhile," had been the response to one of my questions. I wasn't as irritated with this person as I had been a few months ago.

I was almost done looking through the papers when I saw a large blue sticky note, stuck to the back of the last paper. "I'm not sure if I have really been as good a friend as I had wanted to be or if I was a good example. But my life was changed as I tried to help change someone else's. I do know for certain that you were the only person who could have changed your future. And I believe that you did. You deserve the 'A' I gave you. I am going to miss having someone to talk to," it read.

Neither my partner nor I chose to reveal ourselves after the project had ended. Even after reading the note, I still was relieved that anonymity had been kept. I never wanted that person to be able to place my most personal thoughts and feelings with a face.

I threw the folder in my backseat again, deciding that since Mrs. Flint had gone to such trouble, even trash digging to get it for me, the least I could do was keep it for a few days.

Twenty-Three

It was getting close. The hotter the days became the worse things would get. Every other year things seemed way more hopeless. We would ignore it when she would walk around the house clinging to that worn out tiny blue blanket. I wondered if this year things were going to be different. My mom was laughing more than I had ever heard her in the month of June, but she still couldn't hide the hint of sadness that crept in on her every now and then.

The day before Bryce's sixteenth birthday, she was in the kitchen baking as I made myself a sandwich. B.J. had just gotten to our house. "What are you boys planning on doing today?" my mom asked.

"I kind of wanted to go to an arcade," B.J. said. "Do you want to do that?" He looked at me smiling.

"Sure, I guess so," I said.

"Where is one?" he asked

I didn't answer.

"There's only one in the city, it's off Main Street," my mom said. She looked at me and then said, "You remember, don't you Jared? We used to take you there all the time when you were little."

I remembered all right.

"Do you need help with anything, before we leave?" I asked instead of answering her question.

My mom pulled some cookies from the oven and placed them on the counter by our telephone only to stop as soon as she saw the calendar hanging on the wall next to it. She grabbed the pen hanging from it and slowly crossed off the thirteenth of June. She had drifted off in her own world.

B.J. watched her with a concerned look on his face. He went to touch her shoulder but I stopped him. "Mom," I said quietly. "Is it okay if I go to the cemetery with you tomorrow?"

She pried her eyes from the calendar to look at me. "You want to go with me?" she cried.

"Yes, would that be okay?"

"Sure," she smiled and then gave me a hug. She held me tightly like she was trying to absorb some kind of strength from me that I didn't have.

"I'm going to be there, too."

She let go to look at B.J. "You don't have to go," she said.

"Yes, I do," he answered slowly.

My mom grabbed B.J.'s hand as she said, "I won't stop you. You are a part of this family, also."

"You guys are the family I've always known I could have," B.J. said.

My mom was wiping her eyes with the sleeve of her shirt as she said, "I'm being such a baby. You boys go ahead and have some fun." She shooed us away with her hands.

ꙮ

"Which is your favorite?" B.J. asked me. He grabbed the joystick of the game closest to him and started pushing the blue and red buttons next to it. I wound my way through the arcade until I found the hunting game with two bright orange plastic rifles.

It had always been my favorite. I never wanted to play anything else. "This one," I said.

"How do you play?" he asked as soon as he got to it.

We played that game for three hours straight.

"My pointer finger is sore." I laughed as I moved it back and forth.

"That game is intense," B.J. said with a straight face.

I sat on the seat of a racing game to relax. B.J. was still looking at the hunting game when he asked, "Was that the game you wanted to play with your brother?"

I got uncomfortable. "You really know how to make things awkward, don't you B.J.," I said trying to laugh.

B.J. just looked at me until I answered, "Yes, yes it was."

Then he smiled. "I don't blame you. That was a fun game."

"Yes it is," I said slowly.

"Your dad didn't mean it."

"Excuse me?" I said quickly.

"I don't believe that he meant those things he said to you here that day."

"What did he mean then?" I also had started to think that maybe he didn't want to shatter me, but that he thought he was helping me. I only started coming to this conclusion recently, ever since I had put more of an effort into our relationship.

"I think he distanced himself from the pain, and he wanted you to do the same."

I knew now that B.J. was probably right. After talking to my dad at my Grandpa's funeral, I realized that he wanted me to handle the situation like he did and not like my mom. He was numb to it, or at least he tried to convince himself that he was.

"He did it, because with every mention of Bryce's name, my dad would feel something. The pain of grief would briefly replace his numbness. My naïve view made him hurt more," I said, explaining for the first time what I had failed to see for so long.

B.J. put the plastic rifle he had been holding back on its stand.

"It's starting to get late," I said after a while; it was nine o'clock at night and the room we were in no longer seemed happy to me. "Should we go?"

B.J. looked at the game one last time and then said, "We probably should."

"This was a pretty good idea," I said as we pulled off Main Street. "I actually had fun."

"So it wasn't too bad spending three hours with me?" B.J. teased.

"I survived it at least." I laughed.

"You should probably put on your seat belt because the night isn't over."

I looked at B.J. and then at my unlatched seat belt, "You're as bad as my mom," I said as I put it on.

A few minutes later B.J. asked seriously, "Have I been a good friend to you?"

"What kind of question is that?" I started to get suspicious.

"I was just wondering," B.J. said quietly. And that was when I saw it. He had quickly glanced behind my seat. I turned around and saw the manila folder.

"Are you serious!?" I yelled. "Don't tell me you were my partner all along ... don't say it," I rambled.

"I should have said something sooner," B.J. said.

I slammed my palm into the steering wheel. "How could you! I wrote private things and you, you took advantage of me and my family!" I screamed.

B.J. was gripping the door handle. "It's not like that," he said. "It's not what you think."

"I gave you a second chance. We took you in and made you a part of our family. You lied to me." I had lost it.

"Is withholding information the same thing as lying?" he asked.

"Yes!"

"Then I need to tell you something," B.J. said, his body was tense and he looked like he was almost cringing.

"I don't want to hear anymore from you," I said, my voice was husky from screaming, "except, who you really are."

B.J. looked over at me. His head was shoved against the head rest. "I'm your brother, Bryce."

I stared at B.J. as my body went cold. Then everything went bright. I couldn't see his face anymore. I tried to squint and still couldn't see anything but then I started to make out two distinct circles. I remember thinking that they almost looked like headlights, that was just before my body was jerked forward and then violently slammed back into my driver's side door.

Twenty-Four

"Jared, open your eyes ... focus on me. Everything is going to be fine."

I slowly opened my eyes. My dad was kneeling in front of me. He held my face in his hands.

"You are fine. You just have a cut on your head ... it wasn't your fault, you don't need to worry, son."

A burly police officer with a thick brown mustache pulled my dad aside.

"Before you got here, he was hysterical. He kept rambling on about a brother or something. I managed to get him to calm down enough to give me a number to call. Then he passed out," I heard him say.

My ears were ringing and my vision was blurry, the bright flashing lights on top of the police car weren't helping.

"I'm so sorry." said a young blonde woman. She was standing next to an old Volkswagen. "My brakes just stopped working. I am just so sorry," she cried.

"Let's give him some space," the police officer said as he directed the woman away, but not before he turned to me and said, "You're lucky you didn't have a passenger with you or else someone could have been seriously injured."

My dad had knelt back in front of me. My mouth was open but no words were coming out. I jumped to my feet and ran to the passenger side of the car.

"You really should stay sitting, an ambulance is coming to check you out just in case," I heard my dad say.

The entire passenger door was dented in and I couldn't see the seat anymore. I stuck my hand through the broken window and moved my hand back and forth frantically trying to feel for something. All I felt was glass stabbing me. My dad grabbed me from behind and pulled my bloody hand out.

I started screaming, "Where is he? Where did he go?"

"That is exactly what he was doing earlier," the police officer told my dad as he dragged me from the street to the sidewalk.

"Get a hold of yourself," he yelled in my face. "You need to breathe."

I plopped down on the ground and shoved my head in between my knees.

"Who are you talking about?" my dad asked.

"B.J.," I sobbed. "He was right there in the car with me. Now he's gone."

"No, he wasn't," my dad said adamantly.

"How can you say that," I said. "He was with me, in my car!" I started screaming again. "Oh no, he's dead! He's dead!"

My dad grabbed me from under the shoulders and lifted me up. "Stop this!" he yelled. "You are in shock. You need to calm down and breathe normally."

After I had stopped screaming my dad said, "You just think he was with you because you just experienced a trauma. B.J. was at our house when I got the phone call from the police officer."

"What?" I said. I couldn't believe any of it. It felt like I was in a dream or a horror movie. "How?"

"He came by to drop off a manila folder. He said it was yours," my dad explained. "He also wanted me to tell you that he enjoyed going to the arcade."

I shut my eyes tightly. I couldn't think straight. *Had I completely lost my mind?* "How hard did I hit my head?" I asked.

"We are not sure. The paramedics are going to need to check you out."

"I think I am having memory problems," I said slowly.

"You're going to be fine," my dad said as he patted my back. It felt good having him there. I needed someone to talk sense into me since I was clearly losing it. I remembered distinct details of B.J. being in the car right before we were hit. Now, I didn't even know if the whole confrontation over him being my psychology partner was real or not. But the manila envelope in the backseat had been very real. There was no getting around that.

As the ambulance pulled up behind the cop car, and as the police officer and my dad walked me over to the opened rear doors I strained my mind trying to understand what was real. B.J.'s words, "I'm your brother," kept replaying in my brain like a broken record. I knew that I had to have made that up for sure. I figured that I must have just been thinking about Bryce because his birthday was the next day.

We didn't get home until close to eleven. The paramedics said that I seemed fine, but suggested I go to the hospital to be sure. After a CAT scan and some other tests, they released me.

"Just so you know, your mother is not handling this well," my dad warned me before he opened the front door. I knew she was worried sick but I also knew why she couldn't bring herself to meet my dad and me at the hospital. It was just too hard.

"Of all days I could have gotten into a serious accident, it had to be today," I mumbled.

"There is nothing you could have done to prevent it, but the timing couldn't have been any worse," he agreed.

ℰ𝒪

I felt lightheaded and nauseous at the same time, and it had nothing to do with my car accident the night before. I sat in the back seat of my mom's car, holding my stomach.

"What is taking Lynn so long?" my mom asked.

I didn't answer. I was afraid I would either scream or cry.

My mom had a vase full of purple carnations and that soft blue baby blanket sitting on the passenger side seat. I stared at them.

"I place purple carnations in the most random places sometimes, because it makes her smile." Tears spilled from my eyes as I recalled a part of B.J.'s letter to me.

I could see my mom through the review mirror, her eyes were still bloodshot and I hated thinking about how the night before she had been so scared. The minute I had walked into the house she had collapsed before she could reach me. "Please, never do that to me again," she sobbed at my feet. I picked her up and held her as she cried into my chest.

Lynn walked up to the car, pulling me from my daydream. She was holding a camera. "What's that for?" my mom asked.

"Just in case we want to take a family picture," she said, as she settled into her seat. My heart was beating out of control. I looked at her and she gave me a knowing smile and then put her head on my shoulder. "Lynn knows. She has since Grandpa's funeral," B.J. had written. I thought back to when I had seen B.J. and Lynn talking near the casket. They had been deep in conversation; Lynn had been crying as B.J. rubbed her back softly.

My mom was pulling out of the driveway when my dad came running up to the car. She stopped, unrolled the window, and asked if everything was all right with him. "Can I go with you?" he whispered. My mom quickly covered her mouth and her shoulders started to shake. She nodded her head. My dad looked like he was on the verge of breaking down, too. We had all had a couple of emotional days.

After I had gotten home from the hospital and spent some time calming my mom down, I didn't think things could get crazier. I went to my room and found my manila folder with the number fourteen on it, lying on my bed. I still didn't know how B.J. had gotten it. The doctors had told me that it might take a while to get parts of my memory back.

I opened it and found that all of the papers I had flipped through a few weeks earlier were gone. The blue sticky note and a handwritten letter were the only things in it.

I read B.J.'s letter more than once. I couldn't grasp what he was telling me. It was impossible. "I am your brother. I am Bryce," he had written. It was the same thing I had thought he had said to me before disappearing into thin air.

I didn't know what to do, or who to talk to. I resisted the urge to call Derek. I knew that he had the means to help me forget my life for a few hours. I called Payton instead. "I am going through something difficult right now," was all I had dared to tell her.

"Tomorrow is a big day for your family," she said remembering Bryce's birthday. "It is going to hurt, but I am here for you."

I had confessed to her my weakness, how I contemplated drinking away my worries and escaping from the pain.

"I will not abandon you," she had said. "You have the option to relapse, like Mrs. Flint had talked about, or you have the opportunity to talk on the phone to me all night long. I will help you work through this."

She had stayed on the phone with me until I had fallen asleep.

"Has anyone heard from B.J.?" my mom asked. My chest physically hurt. I bit my lips and refused to look anywhere but out my window.

"Maybe he is already there?" Lynn said quietly. She squeezed my arm.

"Maybe." My mom sounded unsure. "He just sounded like he really wanted to go."

We drove to the cemetery as a family for the first time in ten years. My mom pulled into a parking space and we walked along the path. My dad looked nervous, but held onto my mom's hand as she led us off the path.

My mom took the flowers and blanket from my dad and walked slowly up to the headstone.

"Where's B.J.?" Lynn whispered.

I looked around, but didn't see him.

We watched my mom as she set the vase reverently in the flower pot next to the engraved stone. She knelt down and placed her right hand on the grass above where my brother was buried and she rested her left hand on her heart. Then she cried.

My dad bowed his head and kept rubbing his hands together. He looked like he was trying to hold everything in, suppress every feeling he wanted to feel. He just needed to let go and allow himself to feel human. He suddenly looked up and like he had read my mind, he went to kneel by my mom. He wrapped his arms around her as she gently touched the stone.

I wanted to give them some privacy and as I was getting ready to walk back to the dirt road, B.J. walked out from behind the large pine tree.

"B.J.," Lynn squealed. She ran up to him and wrapped her arms around his neck. He held her tightly. "Mom, Dad ... B.J.'s here," she called.

I couldn't keep from staring. I saw him differently. I used to wonder what Bryce looked like, I guess I know now. He was watching me. Electric shocks filled my feet and legs. "Nothing about life is easy ... but if you do it right, it's worth it," he whispered to both Lynn and me.

My mom and dad had stood as B.J. walked closer to the headstone. Lynn still clung to B.J. I just stared. "Jared, B.J., can I take a picture of you two?" Lynn asked.

I felt dazed. Lynn had been given more time to process the truth, but right then my reality felt like a fantasy. I stood next to B.J. and tried to smile as she took the picture.

"That one's going on our wall for sure," my mom said as she rubbed B.J.'s back. "I really appreciate you coming here today, it means a lot."

B.J. looked almost upset. I didn't understand why until he finally said, "I have to go."

Both Lynn and I looked at each other, then back at B.J.

"Well, we will be leaving here in a few minutes. You are welcome to come over for dinner tonight," my mom said.

"I have to leave you guys," he said, his voice was barely audible.

It seemed like we were all just watching B.J., unable to realize what he was saying. He started to cry and Lynn began shaking her head, "No!" she kept saying.

My parents were confused. I could barely look at my mom, I knew what was coming.

"Jared, you're going to have to get better at math, Lynn needs a tutor." B.J. tried to smile.

"You can't do this to us," I pleaded.

"Please don't stop talking about me, don't stop saying my name. And because I can't, will you live my life for me ... with no regrets?" he asked.

I couldn't hold it in any longer.

"That's not fair," I cried. "I didn't know it was you! I didn't get enough time. If I would have known, I would have ..." I couldn't finish; I completely broke down.

My mom's mouth opened, but she couldn't speak. She looked from me back to B.J. in disbelief as reality slowly hit her. She looked like she might collapse and before my dad or I could get to her, B.J. wrapped her in his arms.

"I get to finally hold my baby boy, again." She started to sob. I watched them for a long time. They held each other, neither one of them willing to let go. "There was always something very special about you," my mom finally said. "In a way I think I knew all along. A mother just knows." she grabbed his face and held it in her hands. She stroked his hair and they both cried.

"Kate, what's going on?" my dad whispered. "This isn't him, it can't be."

My mom grabbed my dad's hand and gently pulled him closer to her and B.J. "Look at him, it's our son," she said. "You can feel it in here." She let go of my dad's hand and touched her chest. And with her right hand she touched B.J.'s chest. "I'll always be your mom," she said to him, and then she kissed him on the cheek. B.J. pulled a single purple carnation from his pocket and placed it in her hand as she let go of him and stepped away. A tiny moan escaped her lips as I walked up to her. I could see how much it hurt her. I held her tightly.

B.J. turned to my dad. "Son?" my dad asked. He looked scared and unsure.

"Dad, I love you," B.J. said. "I know how badly you are hurting, especially when you act like everything is fine." My dad stared blankly for a minute and then grabbed B.J. and held him tightly. I had never seen him cry so hard.

"I was not gone forever," B.J. said to him. "I live just like you guys, just somewhere else and with a lot of other people who love you. I was allowed to come help reunite my family, but now I have other work to do. But I will be with you guys again."

Lynn grabbed B.J. around the waist as soon as my dad had left to stand by my mom and me. He grabbed my mom's hand. "I'm going to miss you B.J.," Lynn said. "You were my only friend."

"I'm going to miss you, too, but you don't need me here with you," B.J. said as he ruffled her hair. "You have Jared and I'm always with you, as are Grandpa, Grandma and a bunch of other people looking out for you."

"I know," she said. She squeezed him one last time before joining my parents.

A million things were going through my mind, keeping my voice from working. B.J. embraced me and whispered into my ear, "Please don't try to understand it. You're not meant to. You don't need proof, you just need to feel." That same warm current filled my body, calming me. "Just remember that even when you can't see me, I am still with you. I am still your brother."

"I love you, Bryce," I said as I pulled the green Robin mask, my mom had made, from my pocket and balanced it on top of his headstone. I walked back to the pathway. Bryce still stood next to his headstone. It was like we knew something incredible was about to happen. I waited anxiously.

"No regrets," was the last thing Bryce said as a bright light surrounded his entire body. The light slowly widened, I could see people everywhere behind and around him. I saw Grandpa and Grandma. He walked behind B.J. and placed his hand on his shoulder. Grandpa smiled and then winked, his arm was around Grandma. Lynn giggled and my mom blew them a kiss and mouthed, "I love you." Within seconds the light started to retract and people started to disappear. B.J. smiled as he started to fade from our view.

There was just a sliver of light left as I joined my family near the dirt road. My heart was broken with having to say goodbye, but strangely lifted in knowing that it wasn't permanent. I guess both he and Payton were right. Before we had gotten too far I glanced back and all I could see was a tiny white speck in a field of green.

About the Author

JAMIE LYNN YEAGER has always had a passion for writing and dreamed of writing novels from the time she was twelve years old. Besides devoting most of her time chasing her children around, Jamie uses her Interior Design background in helping with her family's wedding decorating business. Being a wife and mother of four can be very demanding, but she will always find time for soccer, reading, chocolate chip cookie dough ice-cream, and Pinterest.

Made in the USA
San Bernardino, CA
12 June 2013